The Seventh Stone

Sallie Gabree

VANTAGE PRESS
New York

This is a work of fiction. Any similarity between the characters appearing herein and any real persons, living or dead, is purely coincidental.

Cover design by Susan Thomas

FIRST EDITION

Published by Vantage Press, Inc.
419 Park Ave. South, New York, NY 10016

Manufactured in the United States of America
ISBN: 0-533-14652-6

Library of Congress Catalog Card No.: 2003093842

0 9 8 7 6 5 4 3 2 1

To my husband for the endless hours of writing skills and support he provided for me.

To my granddaughter, Pam, for her inspiration, and to the rest of the family for putting up with me throughout the process.

Contents

Foreword

Sallie Gabree slipped into our lives with her gifts of surprising talent, gentle wit, and quiet determination with little fanfare. My husband and I soon came to treasure the visits with Sallie and her husband, Ed, over a number of years and three states.

In between the visits we found pleasure in sharing Sallie's Christmas card cartoons with our family and friends. Each card reflected the location of the Gabrees—an alligator from Florida, for example. Oh, but *such* an alligator—his spectacular toothy grin heralding the season kept us all laughing well into January. So, we knew Sallie was an artist.

Then she surprised us with a book—more talent on display from this lady. My years of teaching help me welcome such a book full of delights for children—elfin creatures, magical people, animals able to speak and do wondrous things. Such books can carry our children and us along with them to delightful places so much easier to inhabit than a world unpleasantly real for us today.

Take this journey Sallie has created. You'll find it's rather like celebrating Christmas with a silly, toothy alligator, unreal and wonderful.

—Mary LaPanse, Ed.D.

The Seventh Stone

Prologue

This is a story about the Kingdom of Grindle. It is found only by discovering the key to the seventh stone, which is located to the right of the circle of the "Ring of Stones" situated somewhere in the meadows of southern England. In order to find the seventh stone, one must determine which of the stones in the circle is the first one. The answer is hidden in a book called *The Seventh Stone.*

1
The Letter

Robert Penny woke with a start, spilling the cup of coffee that was sitting on the tray in front him. He was returning to New York, after his trip to London, when the drone of the jumbo jet's engines put him to sleep. He quickly mopped up the coffee with some tissues when the attendant brought a wet towel to finish the job, along with a new cup of coffee.

As he sipped the hot coffee, he stared out the window onto the tops of the fluffy clouds, his thoughts going back to the beginning, wondering if it had all been a dream, until he felt that familiar tingling sensation in his jacket pocket. . . .

The Tower Shop, a 19th century bookstore, was situated on Pickwick Street, a few blocks from London's famous Tower. The shop had been closed after old Mr. Penny died and had been left to his great nephew, Robert Penny.

Robert lived in New York City in a modest apartment on the West Side. He was nearing forty, divorced and was one of five accountants in the H.M. Motley accounting firm. This was his third year there, and about the only excitement he had was looking forward to the beginning of each year when the business picked up during tax time.

His co-workers kidded him about how dull and unadventurous his life was. He did have a girlfriend, Katie, who would occasionally meet him for dinner and a movie. Katie worked in the Egyptian Room at the City Museum, along with Robert's high school buddy Sam, who—according to Robert—was a one-of-a-kind character.

One morning after pouring a cup of coffee, Robert sat at the table in his kitchen nook, which faced the front door. As he sipped his coffee, he noticed an envelope sliding under the door. He quickly went to the door and opened it, but no one was there. After searching the hall, he returned to his apartment, picked up the envelope and closed the door. It was addressed to Robert C. Penny. The return address was from a Solicitor Redding, 1340 Chelsey Street, London.

Robert opened the envelope and unfolded the paper. He noticed the crispness of the paper and its light rainbow sheen. He read, "Your presence is requested at Solicitor Redding's office on May 14th at 10:30 A.M. for the reading of the will of Mr. Charles Penny." Making airline reservations at this late date would be a costly matter; the 14th was only a week away. He would have to contact Mr. Redding and explain that other arrangements would have to be made. He laid the envelope on the kitchen table, picked up his briefcase and left for work.

Two days went by and Robert gave little thought to the letter. On the third day, he came home from work and while putting that day's mail on the table, he noticed that the letter, which had been sitting there, seemed to have developed a shimmering glow. Astonished at this, he picked it up and looked inside. The printing seemed to be disappearing and the paper was beginning to disintegrate into silver and gold looking shreds.

"What is happening with this?" he said aloud to himself, as he quickly wrote down the name and address of Mr. Redding. He decided that maybe he should go to London after all.

He called the airline to make reservations. Fortunately, he had a passport that he had secured the year before for a vacation, which had been cancelled because of work. When he got to the office, he notified his supervisor of his upcoming trip, which posed no problem since tax time had just ended, and things had slowed down considerably.

Robert called Katie at the museum and told her of his plans. She had just received a recently discovered mummy from Egypt, so she would be quite busy for a few weeks anyway. He then packed clothes, enough for what he thought would be only a week or two.

2
Grindle

In another time and another place lies a Kingdom tucked into a valley. In the distance, waterfalls cascade down from cliffs into sparkling blue pools so clear that the colorful pebbles lying on the sandy bottom were easily seen. Thick vines with unknown species of flowers hang from the cliffs in profusion giving a heavenly scent of perfume. On the other side of the valley lies a meadow stretching far into the horizon giving one a sense of infinity. A great castle stands majestically, surrounded by the village of Grindle in the center of the valley facing the meadows.

There was a celebration in the Kingdom, for it was to be the crowning of William, the Crown Prince. William's father, the former King, had, according to the rules of the land, reached the age of three hundred and fifty, and was no longer allowed to rule. Therefore, his son William was declared to be the next in line to become King. However, the old King had a younger brother, Grizzard, who was the Kingdom's Wizard. Being only two hundred years old, the Wizard thought that he should be King, and was really ticked off when the old King chose his own son, William, instead because he was younger still—a mere 100 years old.

The people of Grindle had been busily preparing for the festivities for weeks and the time had finally arrived.

They gathered together in the town square, which was elaborately decorated with garlands of flowers and potpourri scents, along with the vendors and musicians, anxiously awaiting the arrival of the Wizard Grizzard, who by tradition would place the crown upon the head of the new King.

The trumpets blared and the Wizard Grizzard rode into the square on his powerful black horse, looking very wizard-like in a long colorful robe and a tall peaked hat. He had a long white beard, wore rings on his fingers and carried a tall magical staff. He also carried the book that held all the secrets and magic that enveloped the land of Grindle. It was tradition that the book was held by the future King as he was being crowned. The Wizard dismounted from his horse and, with his robe flowing behind him, walked with long strides to the center of the square, in front of the great fountain of Grindle.

Again, the trumpets sounded and the crowd cheered as William entered the square on his beautiful, prancing white horse. He looked quite handsome and the Wizard glared at him with envy. Following William, riding a majestic brown horse, rode the old King in all his finery, wearing the gold crown that would soon sit on the head of the new King.

William dismounted his horse. He was dressed all in white with a cape embroidered in gold. He proceeded to the center where the Wizard was standing.

The old King, who was now standing beside William, lifted the crown from his head and placed it into the hands of the Wizard. The trumpets blared again as the Wizard handed the book to William. Looking at the crown which he thought should be his, Grizzard held it high in the air. William kneeled down for him to place it on his head, but instead, the Wizard placed it upon his own head. The sky turned dark. Lightning and thunder filled the air.

The crowd gasped and William rose in disbelief, reaching for the crown. "Never will you be King of Grindle!" the Wizard bellowed. "I banish you to another world, another time and another form in which you shall live for eternity!" He then reached up with his staff, bringing lightning from the sky and, with it, touched William. But as the lightning hit William, it bounced, hitting the book he held. Bouncing again, it then hit the Kingdom Witch Hilga, who at the time happened to be flying by at the top of the castle walls. As it hit Hilga, it bounced again, hitting a gargoyle on the castle behind her. And all three, along with the book, were transported to the time and place the Wizard spoke of. . . .

3
Another Time and Place

There was a light mist as the plane touched down, which Robert understood to be typical English weather. After leaving the airplane, he walked with the other two hundred or so passengers to the area where he retrieved his luggage and cleared customs. His next step was to exchange American dollars into pounds. He then checked the train schedule to London's Victoria Station and found one leaving in fifteen minutes, which he would be able to catch if he hurried. He boarded the train just as it was beginning to roll. He selected a seat near the window so he could relax and enjoy the scenery.

The English countryside was just like the pictures he'd seen. Cows dotted the meadows and hedges separated one parcel of land from another. There was an occasional village along the way, where the train would make a quick stop to pick up passengers going into London.

Robert found a hotel not far from the train station. Luckily there was a room available. He checked in and unpacked his bag. Jet lag was taking over, so he took a shower and, lying on the bed, quickly went to sleep. He awoke several hours later and decided that since this day was the 13th and it was only 1:30 P.M., he would go out and do some sightseeing. He walked a couple blocks and found a pub where he went in to have a cool drink and a sandwich. He met some of the locals and enjoyed their conversations. This was the first he'd been away from work in a long time and he was beginning to relax and enjoy it. Leaving the pub, he caught a double-decker bus and rode from one end of the city to the other, stopping now and then to visit places of interest. With so much history and wonderful architecture, he decided he would like to spend more time in England, perhaps in the future with his friend Katie.

Later he returned to the hotel and took the envelope from his briefcase. The letter had totally crumbled into silver-and-gold dust. *What is this stuff?* he wondered. He carefully closed the envelope and hoped that at the reading of the will with Mr. Redding, things would be explained. After a light dinner in the hotel dining room, he went to bed early.

The next morning, Robert woke early, anxious about his meeting with Mr. Redding. He had an hour or so to spare, so decided to walk to a coffee shop he'd seen the day before. He went in and ordered a cup of coffee. Drinking slowly and watching the other patrons, he noticed an elderly man, wearing a very old-looking coat entering the shop with a newspaper tucked under his arm. The man wore tattered shoes on large long feet. Robert thought that those feet were much too long for the size of the person he was looking at. Walking hunched over, he had the weathered look of a man who had lived a hard, labor-filled life. As a matter of fact, he looked as though he'd just stepped out of a Charles Dickens novel.

The man stopped in front of Robert, looked piercingly into his eyes and handed him a crumpled piece of paper which created a tingling sensation in Robert's fingers. The old man then nodded and sat down at a table in the back of the coffee shop.

Robert uncrumpled the paper and read: THE PIECES OF THE PUZZLE ARE ONLY THREE—PUT THEM TOGETHER AND THERE IT WILL BE.

What the heck is that? he thought as he looked toward the back of the shop. But the old man had disappeared. Robert finished his coffee, paid at the counter and went outside. He walked another half block to a taxi stand and gave the driver the address of the Solicitor's office. The cabbie drove through narrow and curvy streets to the address furnished him.

"Hmm," said the driver. "I thought there was a boutique and flower shop on this corner. Must be getting forgetful."

Robert paid the fare, thanked him and stepped out onto the sidewalk.

The Solicitor's office was in a quaint old building with gargoyles hanging over the door. Robert entered and looked around at the furnishings that appeared old and antique. Suddenly and quietly, an old gentleman appeared from a back room. He was short, stout, balding, wore thick eyeglasses and moved with quick jerks and frequently looked at his pocket watch. Motioning for Robert to sit down, he said, "Good day, Robert, I've been expecting you."

Robert, surprised that the man knew who he was, said, "You know who I am, even though you've never seen me before?"

"I was expecting you at ten-thirty and you're here so you must be Robert, right? Sit, sit."

"Yes, sir," Robert said as he obediently sat down at the table, with the old man sitting at the opposite end.

"I'm Syms Redding," the old man said. "I was a friend of and Solicitor for your Uncle Penny would you like some tea."

"Oh, no thank you," said Robert, thinking what a strange little man this was. He ran all of his words together in the same sentence, non-stop, and he kept looking at his pocket watch, reminding him of the White Rabbit in *Alice in Wonderland.* Robert kept looking at the door, expecting others to come in, maybe the March Hare, or the Dormouse—but no one did.

"Am I the only heir to Uncle Penny's will?" Robert now asked.

"Why, yes, you are, what did I do with that deed oh here it is your uncle Penny had a bookstore over on Pickwick Street he left it to you it has been closed for several months since Mr. Penny died," said Mr. Redding, catching his breath.

Robert watched Syms Redding fumbling with the papers and then lifting a brown envelope from underneath the stack. He took a large brass key from it and handed it to Robert.

"The store is yours but first sign the papers here that I've laid out before you then you can be on your way."

Robert signed the papers placed before him, noticing that they had the same iridescent sheen as the letter.

"I was wondering, Mr. Redding, about these papers and the letter I received from you. They seem the same. And the letter crumbled into nothing. Why was that?"

Mr. Redding mumbled something as he fumbled with the brown envelope that had contained the key. Robert looked at the key and thought how much it looked like the old skeleton keys used long ago. His hand tingled now with that same mysterious sensation as the note paper had provoked. He put the key back into the brown envelope and put it, along with the copies of the signed papers, into his briefcase. He looked up, waiting for a clear explanation of the disappearing paper, but Mr. Redding was slipping through the back door he'd previously come out of. As he was leaving, he suddenly turned around and said to Robert, "By the way—the bookstore comes with a cat named William." He closed the door and was gone.

Robert stood a few minutes musing at Mr. Redding's bewildering mannerisms, then picked up his case and left the office. The sky was clouding up and it had started to mist. He hailed a cab and gave him the address on Pickwick Street. The cab zigzagged through the narrow streets, turning many corners, in what seemed to be a maze of side streets. The store fronts had the look of the old times. The timbers framing windows and doors were of old, warped wood with iron hinges and handles, and most of the street's buildings looked as though they leaned a little. The streets were cobblestone, giving the picture a look of quaintness.

Robert had lost his sense of direction some time ago. Finally the driver stopped in front of another store, with the Charles Dickens's look of *Olde Curiosity Shop*. The sign above the door read, "The Tower Book Shop." It swung on the same-looking large hinges attached to a black iron frame. The door was large and quite old and in need of some paint and general repair. It had a window on the right side of the door, and two windows on the left side, with small glass panes in leaded framework. Robert took the brass key from the envelope and slid it into the wrought iron latch on the door. It made a clunking sound as it turned.

"There is also a cat named William?" *What will I do with a cat? Besides, it probably isn't here anymore, since no one has been around for several months. And, how would a cat have survived this long locked up here?* He was hoping he would not find a dead cat somewhere inside.

Robert pushed open the heavy wooden door and stepped into the shop, which was dark and musty. His steps echoed as he walked on the wooden floor. He left the door open for fresh air and opened the shuttered windows to let in more light. On the right side of the room, near the door, was a counter with a marble top that held an old-fashioned cash register. The room was large with a railing separating the counter area from the shelves and tables which were strewn with books. On the left side of the room was a staircase that led to a loft overlooking the rest of the store. Robert could see more books stacked on more tables up there. Along with the floating dust were cobwebs hanging all over.

What a mess, he thought. *This is going to take some work.*

Placing his briefcase on the counter next to the cash register, he walked to the back of the room where he found a door to a smaller room that had a table, chair, sink—and yet another door. Robert unlatched and opened the door, which led to the alley in back of the store. It had a small makeshift space between the door and frame, which appeared to be big enough for a cat to come and go. He hoped that this would perhaps explain how the cat (if there was one) might have survived this length of time. He shut and latched the door and walked back out into the shop area. He couldn't shake a weird feeling that he wasn't totally alone, but tried to ignore it by making a quick assessment of what might be needed for repairs and general cleaning the place would require. He wasn't sure yet what he was going to do with a bookstore in London while he lived in New York, but in the meantime, it would have to be prepared for sale if that's what he decided to do. Going out of the store, he locked the door and put the key into his pocket. Earlier in the day, he'd noticed a small hardware store just a few blocks down the street, so thought he would see if they had what he needed. He enjoyed the walk and nodded to passers-by as they nodded to him. He kept noticing their clothing, which looked of another era.

Robert read "Chadwick's Hardware Store," printed on the window as he opened the door and stepped inside. He thought how everything looked as old as the outside. Like traveling back in time. Items were neatly arranged on shelves. Small bins contained small items, such as nails and screws. Large bins were full of what looked like wheel spokes that were used on the old horse-drawn coaches, along with other things he could not identify. On the end of one shelf were paper bags for holding the loose items. Robert picked out a couple dozen nails and an equal number of screws, knowing he would be sure to find a use for all of them. He also picked up a hammer, a broom, a dustpan, and some wood polish to clean and brighten the wooden railings, tables, and chairs.

"Good afternoon, Mr. Penny," said the man behind the counter.

"Good afternoon. Mr. Chadwick, I presume," said Robert. "How did you know my name was Penny?"

"Oh, word gets around quickly here, Mr. Penny. We were all waiting for you to arrive. Your great-uncle and a group of our friends would come into my store and swap tales. He spoke of you often and how he was leaving the bookstore to you in his will. We will miss him." He handed Robert his change from the five-pound note Robert had given to him. He slipped the receipt into the bag of nails and screws.

"Thank you, Mr. Chadwick. I'm beginning to wish I had known him more than I did as a child." Robert said good-bye and left the store. He thought how different everyone he'd met so far seemed to be. As he walked back to the bookstore, he stopped at a small grocery along the way where he purchased some cat food and two small bowls for the cat.

Entering the store, Robert laid everything on the front counter and took the cat food to the room in the back. He opened one of the cans with his knife, since he hadn't thought to buy a can opener, scraped some of the food into one bowl, and poured water from the faucet into the other. He knew he was going to have to make a decision about what to do with the place. He could sell it, or maybe he could hire someone to manage it for him. He would consult with Mr. Redding tomorrow for his thoughts on the subject. With nothing more to be done today, he returned to the hotel to make calls to New York and let Katie know what was happening up to now.

Not considering the time difference, he caught Katie fast asleep. She'd had a long, stressful day at the museum; Robert told her he might have to remain in England longer than originally planned if he decided to sell the shop, and that he looked forward to seeing her soon. Coincidentally, his high school buddy, Sam, worked with Katie in the Mummy department. While Sam was always a little off the wall, he was a true and devout friend.

"Tell Sam hi for me and tell him I'll call him later."

Robert showered, dressed in casual clothes and went to the hotel dining room for dinner. The room was full of locals and tourists. He ate and watched the people wondering about their everyday lives.

4
Zap

A year or so earlier, Prince William had found himself disheveled and dumped on some old boxes somewhere on the streets of London. His appearance had changed some, he was now smaller, had fur and was referred to, by some of the alley cats, as the new cat in town. *Darn that Wizard,* thought William. He was clutching the book, the only chance he had of ever returning to Grindle, but he would have to hide it somewhere until he could figure out what to do. He discovered a door to one of the buildings in the alley that had a piece of wood broken off at the bottom. He managed to squeeze inside and found it to be a room that was in the back of a larger room. *Perhaps a store of some kind*, he thought. He also noticed some old boxes stacked in the corner of the room that looked as though they hadn't been touched for some time. He could hide the book behind them until he could think of a better place. Besides, the place appeared to be deserted.

In the meantime, Hilga, the Kingdom Witch, and the gargoyle both landed in the gardens of Buckingham Palace, where they were roughed up a bit from crashing through an old oak tree.

"You crazy old witch!" yelled the gargoyle. "Why did you have to be flying up there near me? Just look at me! I've got chips on my ears from falling though that tree.

And just what am I supposed to do on the ground? Gargoyles don't usually have legs, you know! And we can't stay here on the palace grounds forever! Jeesh! I was perfectly happy, until you had to be flying . . ."

"Oh, shut up! I will give you some legs!" Hilga grumbled. "Then you can be on your way and me on mine!"

Waving her hands in the air, she blurted, "HOCUS, POCUS, TWIDDLY DEET. MAKE HIM STOP QUACKIN AND GIVE HIM SOME FEET!" The gargoyle was whipped into the air and flipped onto his back. "DUCK FEET? I DON'T WANT DUCK FEET!" snarled the gargoyle between clenched, jagged teeth.

"Well, I don't do legs, you crazy old piece of cement!" Hilga snapped. "Here, I will fix them!"

Again, she sputtered, "TRANSFORM THE DUCK TO A DECOY OF WOOD. ZAP IT, WAP IT, AND NOW MAKE IT GOOD!" This time only one leg was changed. And into wood! A peg leg!

"Oh, oh," said Hilga, crestfallen. "Okay, stand still, I'll try again."

"Don't touch me!" hissed the gargoyle.

"We have to figure out what to do, and how to get back to Grindle," mumbled Hilga, as she walked back and forth. "We can't stay here."

"Just throw your ugly old shawl over me and let's get out of here! I'll hobble around as is for the time being," snarled the gargoyle.

"Well, come along then, let's go before we're caught in the Queen's garden and thrown into the Tower," whispered Hilga, as she picked up the heavy gargoyle and wrapped it in her shawl. "Hang on!" she said as she quickly flew to the top of the stone wall and over to the other side.

"We might as well stick together since we are after

the same goal. And I suppose you might come in handy, for whatever reason," she grudgingly said, as she lowered the gargoyle to the ground, still cloaked in the shawl.

Off they went, Hilga and gargoyle with its one duck foot and one peg leg. *Slap, bonk, slap, bonk.*

5
The Presence

The next morning, Robert took a cab to the café across the street from the bookstore, where he ordered a cup of coffee and a biscuit to go. He then proceeded to the bookstore where he unlocked the door with the large brass key and went in. He had a lot of work to do, so he would start early. He took off his jacket and put the key into his pocket. He pulled out the crumpled piece of paper the old man gave him and threw it on the floor to be swept up later.

He drank the coffee, ate the biscuit and then picked up an old rag he'd found in the back room. With the polish he bought at the hardware store, he started wiping down and rubbing the banisters, finding them to be of beautiful aged wood. He polished, swept, dusted fixtures, wiped down cobwebs, straightened books and nailed loose shelves secure. He put new screws into the gate hinges that separated the counter area from the book area. All the while he worked, he felt as though he was being watched.

After a long and laborious day, the place was beginning to look pretty darn good. The books had a semblance of order and were even categorically organized, to some extent. Robert straightened the counter and set up the receipt books and wrapping material, thinking he might make a few sales in the next week.

The last job was to sweep up the pile of debris that had collected on the floor. As he swept, the small piece of paper he'd thrown on the pile kept falling out. He tried several times to sweep it into the dustpan and each time it would flutter back out onto the floor. He finally reached down to pick it up and it fluttered away from him. He quickly stepped on it with his foot, picked it up and put it into his pocket. A crazy piece of paper with a riddle on it, given to him by a strange old man, seemed to have a life of its own. Might be fun to show it to Katie and Sam.

It was late in the afternoon when Robert finished. He stood at the front door looking back. It still looked like something out of a Dickens novel. In fact, a lot of things lately looked like something out of a Dickens novel.

Suddenly, a slight breeze whisked past his face, giving him shivers. There was that feeling of another presence of something or someone, but of course, there was no one there.

Then suddenly, "It's about time they sent you!"

Robert jumped and turned around. "Hello!" he said, thinking perhaps someone might've come into the store while he was in the back room. "Hello!" he said again. He then walked throughout the store, including the back room and the upstairs loft, searching everywhere.

"I must be hearing things. Probably just the same breeze that wasn't here to flutter that crazy piece of paper," he snickered at himself nervously. He was beginning to feel spooked in these antiquated surroundings. He quickly went out the door, locked it and hailed a cab that always seemed to be waiting at the corner. It was the same driver that he'd had all the other times. *He is always here,* Robert thought.

The next morning he went to his uncle's bank and met with one of the financial advisors, who reopened the old, closed account under the name of "The Tower Shop" with Robert as owner and signer. He was told that old Mr. Penny had a safety deposit box and was asked if he would like to see it. Robert said that he would, so the gentleman disappeared behind a closed door for a moment and when he returned, he had two keys. Robert was led through thick steel doors to the vault and around a corner to a room with an iron gate. The gentleman opened the iron gate and with Robert following, they went to the safety deposit box number Seven.

The man slid one key into the lock and gave Robert the other key, which he in turn slid into a second lock. The keys were both turned at the same time and the little door opened showing the metal box inside. Taking the box from the cubicle, the gentleman led Robert to a small room with a door, and laid the box on the table inside. He said he'd be right outside if needed and abruptly left.

Robert carefully removed the lid from the safety deposit box. He noticed that the remains inside were the same silver and gold-like shreds and dust that were in the envelope from the Solicitor's office. Everything was in a state of disintegration. Robert closed the box and returned it to the gentleman.

"I've got to find out what is happening, and why the letters and papers are turning into this stuff," he said to himself as he went outside the bank.

He caught a cab (same driver), and gave him the address of Solicitor Redding's office, the Solicitor he hoped would give him an understandable explanation. After zipping through the narrow streets, turning here and there, the cab came to a halt.

“This is not the address I gave you, there is no office here; just a boutique and a flower shop,” Robert said.

“Yes sir, it is; it is the very same address. Look there above the door, 1340 Chelsea Street,” said the cab driver.

“But this is a boutique and flower shop, not Solicitor Redding’s office,” insisted Robert.

“Oh, but this boutique and flower shop has been here for some years now,” the cab driver responded defensively.

Robert confirmed the address he’d written on the paper as a result of disintegration of the original letter. But where was the Solicitor’s office? It had been here just three days ago!

“Perhaps you have the wrong address?” the cab driver suggested. “I have no knowledge of a Solicitor’s office being here. I’ll take you back to your hotel, and if you’re interested, there is a nice pub around the corner you might enjoy.”

Robert pushed himself back into the seat as the cab whisked away again through the narrow streets. The vehicle stopped in front of the hotel and Robert got out, paid the fare and stood there watching as the cab continued down the street.

“How’d he know where I was staying? I hadn’t told him! I just don’t understand a lot of things,” Robert said aloud to himself. “My mind is just playing tricks on me. I need to take time off more frequently.” He went to his room and lay down on the bed, where he promptly fell asleep.

6
Willie

Later that evening, he awoke and placed a call to Sam in New York. Again, he had forgotten the time difference and Sam sleepily answered.

"Robert? How're things in the British monarchy? Had lunch with the Queen yet?"

"Listen, Sam, I have a favor to ask of you. I have something I'd like you to analyze. It's a sort of dust and shreds of paper. Would you let me know what you find out. The documents I have received, since getting here, keep disintegrating and turning into this stuff!"

"I'm not quite sure what you just said," mumbled Sam. "But send it along and I will see what I can find out. Now say goodnight."

"Thanks Sam; I'll put this into express mail. You should have it in a couple days. Goodnight." Robert carefully put the envelope contents into his briefcase.

The next morning, Robert found a post office not far from the bookstore, and he sent the fragile shreds to Sam.

The next few days were spent in the store. A lot of curiosity seekers entered and wandered about looking at all the fine old books. Some made purchases, others just browsed. Robert was beginning to enjoy the slower-paced atmosphere. Many of the customers stopped to talk about his uncle Penny. They said they missed him and wished the new owner well, expressing joy about the store opening again.

On Sunday, Robert went to the store to start organizing the loft. There were some new books his uncle had received before he died. They had never been removed from the boxes to be displayed. He brought with him a container of coffee and biscuit from the café near the shop and set them down on the table in the loft. He dusted off an old chair and sat down, propping his feet on the table. Leaning back in his chair, he was about to take a sip of the hot coffee, when he looked up and saw at his table-propped feet, a large yellow and brown cat. The moment he saw the cat, a voice from nowhere said, "Good morning, Robert!"

Startled, Robert jumped, propelling the coffee container and himself backward onto the floor. The cat jumped, darting behind some stacked boxes.

"Who's there!" demanded Robert. He got up, ran down the stairs and searched all through the store. It was that same voice that had spoken before.

"I'm up here. My, but you are a nervous person, you scared me to death!" the voice said.

Robert warily walked from the back room to the front and peered up to the loft. He saw the yellow and brown cat looking down at him, with its head between the railing posts.

"I can't talk to you if you're down there and I'm up here," the cat said. The cat seemed to be talking, but since Robert knew cats didn't talk, he said nervously as he climbed the stairs to the left, "Who are you, and where are you?"

"My name's Willie. I came here a couple years ago. I wandered the streets for a looooong time. Met some real neat cats, ate from garbage cans, slept under doorsteps and had rocks thrown at me when I joined the others in their nightly serenades. I did learn a lot, though. The leader of the bunch taught me to speak cat and in turn, I taught him to speak English. I made a lot of friends, and since they thought William—which is my real name—was too stuffy, they called me Willie. And you are Robert?"

Robert stared at the cat in disbelief.

"Sit down, Robert, you look frazzled. Now then, I am the cat here that is talking to you."

"Cats don't talk," said Robert as he numbly sat down.

"Most cats don't, but I do. Not only in English, but I speak fourteen languages. What would you like to hear? Russian, Portuguese, Chinese, French, German? Right now I'm learning dog, bird, squirrel and cow. That moo stuff is a little complicated though, with a moo moo here and there. In most languages, you know, cats just go 'Mirour, Meooooow,' etc., and dogs go 'Roof, roof, woof, bark, bark!' And the birds—now, there are some interesting tweets, but a *cow*? Moo is moo. Not much you can do with that."

Robert stared at Willie in a glazed-over stare, not believing what he was seeing and hearing.

"I'm glad you are finally here, I have so much to tell you, but not now, it's nap time. These cat naps seem to come on so suddenly. Well, night-night for now, Robert."

Willie turned around and gently curled himself up in the table, tucking his tail under him. Placing his chin on his paws, he shut his eyes.

Robert sat there for what seemed like hours just staring at the sleeping cat. He finally decided to get out of the shop for a while. He was beginning to think that he was hallucinating.

Robert walked several blocks observing the people and stores around him and something was just not quite right. It was as if he stepped back in time, and yet not. Some things seemed okay, such as the pubs and cafés. But then, were they? He excused it all thinking he was tired and just needed a good night's sleep. He caught a cab around the corner and swore it was the same driver as all the other times.

7
Hilga

The next day, Robert took the cab (same driver), to the bookstore. When he went inside, everything seemed normal so he tried to disregard the happenings of the day before, even convinced himself it hadn't happened at all. There were many customers and some sales. He was beginning to enjoy working in the shop and visiting with the people. Even a group of young people came in looking for historical books and other educational literature.

Sometime after lunch, the shop was empty so Robert was tidying the front counter. He put the morning receipts into the bank bag, when he heard, *"Slap, bonk, slap bonk."* Looking up, he came face to face with a strange looking woman. She had bright red hair that hung down from beneath a large floppy hat. Her clothing was definitely old and antique. She wore a long sweater-like garment over a dress that hung to her ankles. She wore high-heeled shoes that she didn't seem to stand in too well, because she wobbled a lot. Hurrying behind her was a strange looking creature. Robert guessed it was a dog, although it he wasn't quite sure. It was making that awful "bonking" sound when it walked. It had some sort of covering on it concealing most of its body.

"Can I help you, Madam?" Robert inquired, enjoying the role of proprietor.

"Why yes, I am looking for a particular book, called *The Seventh Stone,*" she replied. "I understand you carry this book?"

"I don't recall seeing that title," Robert said. "But let me look in the inventory to see if I do have it."

As he reached under the counter, he noticed how haggard-looking she was, and as she turned and hobbled toward a table of books, he saw two black pieces of fabric hanging down beneath that awful looking sweater.

"Oh, you have it, alright!" she said, with a jagged smile as she looked back at him. "And I want it!"

Robert wondered how she was so sure he had the book. As he reached for the inventory list, he felt something fuzzy. He jumped back. Sitting under the counter was that yellow and brown cat with a paw at its mouth.

"Shhh," the cat whispered.

Robert stared at the cat. He then composed himself, grabbed the inventory book and laid it on the countertop. He followed the alphabet to the S's; he saw there was no listing for the book the woman wanted.

"I'm sorry madam. But I don't show it in the inventory. Can I order it for you?"

Willie jumped down from under the counter and slowly crept around to the other side, peering at the woman from the corners of his yellow eyes, as he disappeared into the back room. The strange woman watched Willie as he walked away. Then suddenly, "No! You cannot order it. I know you already have it! It is here somewhere and I will be back for it!" she rudely said. She turned and stomped toward the door with that weird creature scurrying behind her.

Robert rolled his eyes, bent down to put the inventory book back under the counter. When he stood up, there in front of him was Willie. Again, he recoiled in panic.

"You sure are a jumpy person, Robert. You need to relax more. That woman is Hilga; she is a witch and she is looking for me, but she doesn't know it's me yet, and she wants that book and she must not find either of us! I just have to be careful and not let her hear me talking!"

Robert sat down on the stool, rubbed his face with his hands and said,

"By all means, you shouldn't let anyone hear you talking. But I do, so why am I the lucky one?"

"Because you are here to help me, and I will tell you why. But first, you will have to lock the door, no one must come in," said Willie stamping his little paws with excitement. Robert obediently got up, locked the door and sat back down looking at the cat from the corner of his eyes.

8
The Story

Willie began to pace back and forth on the counter. "I have sooooo much to tell you! First of all, I'm not really a cat; I am a prince from a place called 'Grindle,' in southern England. I can't give you exact locations, so don't ask." (Robert wasn't about to ask.) "I am heir to the throne and was almost crowned King when the Wizard Grizzard, who was to crown me, put the crown on his own head and then zapped me, along with that crazy old woman and that lump of stone, 'Gargoyle.' Since I was holding the book that Hilga is looking for, it was transported along with me. That book is VERY important! It holds all the clues to Grindle and I have to have it so I can return there. It is also Hilga's ticket back. But she has to make sure I don't find it first and go back to take the throne away from Grizzard, because he was going to make *her* Head Wizard! She's always wanted to be Head Wizard. Anyway, I hid the book in the back room by way of a small hole in the door, thinking the place was not being used. Your uncle found it; he thought it belonged in the shop and put it away somewhere. I need to find that book. You have to find it for me, Robert!

"Anyway, since I was here, I decided to get acquainted with the alley cats of London. They were quite nice and they showed me the best garbage cans to rummage through. Soon, I became one of them and we did have some good times—still do, as matter of fact," Willie said with a smile.

"One day old Mr. Penny, your uncle, found me having dinner from a can out back and he felt sorry for me, plus since he had a mouse or two, brought me inside and took care of me. He gave me a warm rug in the back under the sink to sleep on. As time went by, we became friends and I told him about myself and about the book, which he put somewhere and had forgotten where. He really wanted to help me return to Grindle, but he died before remembering where he put the book. I think it may be on a shelf in the loft, but of course it's such a mess up there, I haven't any idea where it might be. You really have to clean it up, Robert! Mr. Redding and the Outside People thought that since you were old man Penny's nephew, you would be the perfect one to help me. Therefore, they've been watching you for sometime to see if you were a trusting person and apparently you are, or they would not have sent the letter to you. Not only that, but you see, even though we all speak many languages, we do not read or write. None of us, except Mr. Redding, who wrote the letter to you. But he's back in Grindle now, and I am here, and you are able to read, so you're it! Anyway, I need to tell you and get a load of this, the people of Grindle and myself are," as he held up his two front paws at his shoulders and fluttered them, "FAIRIES!" Willie sat down and waited for his audience of one to respond.

"Well? You are looking really weird, Robert. Do you feel okay? I know a great remedy for ailments, some fairy dust that I just happen to have with me. A little sprinkle and, Voilá!"

Robert looked at Willie and then lay his head on the

counter. *I have to be hallucinating! Maybe when I look up that cat will be gone? No, he's still there.*

". . . Robert?" said Willie.

Looking directly at Willie, Robert began, "Most cats meow and purr."

"Oh, I meow and I have also picked up quite a nice purr, don't you think?"

"Okay," said Robert. "If I am going to have a conversation with you, I have some questions that have to be answered first. Strange things have been happening to me since I got that letter from Mr. Redding! It disintegrated and turned into silver and gold-like dust and shreds. Then Mr. Redding's office was not there when I went back to see him. The will and the ownership papers Redding gave me are beginning to disintegrate into the same stuff as the letter. The cab driver, always the same one by the way, knew where I wanted to go before I could tell him. An old man in the coffee shop gives me a piece of paper with a crazy riddle on it, which keeps jumping out of the dustpan. A crazy looking woman—excuse me, a witch—with red hair, comes in with a weird looking animal she calls 'Gargoyle,' demanding that book you talk about. Then there's you . . . a fairy prince? . . . but then, everything is tied in together, right?"

Willie looked at Robert with drooping eyelids. With a big yawn, he said, "Nap time!" Then, seeing Robert's consternation, he relented.

"Okay, the cab driver is one of our people, called the Outside People, who work for us. The old man, Merlin, is special, he's been around a long time. And hang on to that jumping piece of paper, the riddle will make sense eventually. Hilga is Hilga and that pet she calls 'Gargoyle' really *is* a gargoyle that just happened to be hanging behind her at the wrong time." And with another huge yawn,

Willie mumbled, "Oh, and by the way—the disintegrating papers are RECYCLED FAIRY WINGS."

"WHAT? RECYCLED WHAT?" Robert yelled at Willie, who was already sound asleep. Had the cat said what Robert thought he said?

Robert went over the whole conversation and knew no one in New York would believe him. Well, maybe Sam. But Robert realized he would probably be staying here for a little longer, as there were too many unfathomable occurrences going on to ever leave now. He would have to let Katie and Sam know . . .

There was a message at the front desk from Sam, when Robert arrived at the hotel. "Call me ASAP, Sam." Robert went to his room and put through the call. He didn't even hear the ring when Sam answered.

"What's up, Sam?"

"Robert, where'd you get that stuff you sent?"

"Why?" he hesitantly asked.

"Well, I had one of the boys at the botanist lab at the museum take a look at it, and he could not come up with a comparison to any current plant life, but he works with an entomologist who spends time studying butterflies and he said it compares to butterfly wings, but then again, not quite, and at the same time had components of silver and gold. Robert, are you still there?"

"Fairy wings," Robert said softly.

"Huh? Huh? What'd you say?"

"I'll get back to you Sam. Thanks."

9
The Book

The next day Robert decided it was time to find another place to stay. The hotel was getting quite costly and he had no idea, now, how long he would be in London. He'd noticed earlier, a sign advertising a room for rent above a pharmacy about three blocks from the book shop. He went to the pharmacy and entered. Why did the man behind the counter seem so very familiar? It suddenly occurred to Robert that this man, the cab driver, and Mr. Chadwick, all looked somewhat like Mr. Redding, with only slight differences, such as one had hair, the other didn't. Robert inquired about the room and decided to take it for the rest of his stay, however long that was going to turn out to be. He paid the first month's rent and returned to the hotel to check out.

He moved his belongings to the new room. It had a small area that contained a sink and enough counter space to hold a hot plate for light cooking, which he would probably never do. He spent the rest of the day with the move and did some laundry at a local laundromat. Later he went to the little café he had visited earlier, for dinner. He thought he would check in on Willie at the book store before calling it a day. Willie wasn't around anywhere, but then Robert knew that the cat did come and go as he wished through the hole in the back door.

Robert set out some fresh cat food and water. He never cared much for cats, but was getting a soft spot for this one. After all, how many multi-linguistic cats does one run into? He took a quick tour of the shop and finding everything in order, locked up for the night.

The next day, the sun was shining through the little paned windows of the shop, casting ribbons of light onto the wooden floors. Probably the first real sunshine since Robert arrived.

"Willie! Where are you?" he called. There was no answer, which almost made Robert a little relieved, since cats are not commonly supposed to talk. At least that's what he had previously believed. Willie must still be outside, or asleep somewhere. *He's always sleeping,* thought Robert. He hung the OPEN sign in the window and while early customers were coming in and browsing, he began straightening the loft, from which he was able to see the customers and hear the bell above the door when anyone came into the store. He piled books according to subject matter. He then cleaned the bookshelves and filled them with the stacked books. Some sales were made, so it took him longer than he thought, because of running up and down the stairs and the conversations with the customers as they came in. But he found it pleasing and therapeutic.

The bell tinkled again and something made Robert shiver. There was that sound again! He looked down and saw Hilga, wobbling in with that creature she called "Gargoyle" close behind her. A witch! according to Willie, he chuckled to himself. But Robert looked at her more carefully this time. She did look like a witch, haggard, with that awful red hair. He caught a glimpse of the black fabric hanging down from beneath her sweater in the back. At that moment Willie bounded in from the back room. He saw Hilga and with his tail high in the air, he went over to her and began rubbing against her dress.

"Get away from me, you mangy animal!" the witch hissed.

Willie stepped back, turned around and came face to face with Gargoyle, who in turn, growled and showed its teeth. Willie jumped and went around to the other side of Hilga. Robert came down the stairs, smiled and bid her a good morning. She looked straight at him and her piercing eyes made him shudder. She didn't answer, but continued, followed by Willie, to walk slowly about the main floor examining each book. Robert saw Willie holding up the tips of the black pieces hanging down her back. The cat mouthed the word "Wings," and pointed to them so Robert would see. Robert stifled a laugh and went back upstairs to continue with his work.

Noticing a loose board behind one of the shelves, he went downstairs to get some nails and a hammer from the back room to repair it. He did not see Hilga anymore, so guessed that she had gone, although he hadn't heard the "bonking" sound her bizarre comrade made when it walked. He went back up and pressed the loose board against the wall and tried to hammer a nail into it. The nail sprang out of his fingers and flew across the floor. Retrieving it, he again tried hammering it into the wall. Again it sprang out. Robert tried pressing the board against the wall, but it would not move. He attempted to pull it out a bit to see if something was obstructing it, but again, it did not move.

He squeezed his hand through the opening in the board and felt that strange tingling sensation. He quickly pulled his hand back—and on it was that mysterious silver and gold dust. He reached back in and felt a book that was wedged tightly in place. He needed a flashlight, so he ran downstairs and got it from under the counter. He didn't see Hilga, who was standing behind one of the bookcases, but she saw him and the shiny dust on his hand.

With the flashlight, he climbed the stairs and shined the light into the space behind the loose board. There was the book titled, *The Seventh Stone.* There it was! There actually was a book of secrets, *told to him by a talking cat.* Robert sat down at the table, to regain his composure.

Willie ran up to the loft from the back room and said, "What'd you make of that?" referring to Hilga.

At that moment, they both heard Hilga and Gargoyle walk to the center of the room downstairs, look up and glare at Willie, and then they turned and walked out the front door.

"Oh, oh," said Willie. "Do you think she heard me?"

"I don't know, I didn't know they were still here." Robert answered. "But, guess what, Willie—I found the book!" Willie's eyes got big and he started hopping around.

"Where is it, Robert?"

"I found it behind this old loose board when I tried to nail it back." Robert explained as he took the book out and placed it on the table. "Look, it's all covered with shiny dust."

"That's fairy dust! Quick, open it and let's see what it says. You'll have to read it to me, you know," replied Willie.

Robert carefully opened the cover, exposing the recycled fairy wing pages.

"Why haven't these sheets disintegrated in all this time, like the others?" he asked.

"Because they've been tightly closed within the book covers and kept in the dark behind the wall," explained

Willie. "Now, if they were in Grindle, they would not disintegrate. But here they do."

They both stared at the pages. Robert was amazed at the Olde English, scroll-like, writing on the delicate paper-like material. Willie looked at the indecipherable marks and squealed.

"What does it say? What does it say, Robert? Does it say how I can go back to Grindle? Huh, huh, Robert?"

Robert scanned through the pages. "I don't know yet, Willie. I'm going to have to take time to read this. It looks a little complicated, and again, almost like riddles. It's going to take time," he repeated.

"Well, okay then. I could take a nap, I suppose. I have been out all night with the gang and am a little sleepy. Goodnight, Robert," Willie mumbled as he slowly rested his head on his front paws and immediately fell asleep.

"Wait, Willie! That old man Merlin. Is he . . . ?"

"Is he the old Merlin the Magician? Really, Robert, Merlin the Magician was just a myth in a story of King Arthur. Get a grip!"

" 'Get a grip,' he says. This from a talking cat who claims to be a Fairy King!" said Robert out loud, but Willie, who was fast asleep, didn't hear him.

Robert looked at the glittering dust on his hands and thought, *Fairy Dust.* He shook his head and still had a hard time processing all of this.

He returned the book to the safety of the hidden nook, until later when he could read it without interruption. He then finished the job of organizing the new books on the shelves. He put the empty boxes near the stairs to take down when he went. It was mid-afternoon and he had a few sales that prompted him to run up and down the stairs.

Speaking of Merlin—in came the old man from the

coffee shop, with his big floppy feet and newspaper tucked under his arm. Robert wondered if he actually read the paper. He seemed to browse longer than the rest, looking around the room, watching the other people who came in. He finally departed after an hour without buying anything. It became very quiet later in the day, so Robert locked the front door, put the CLOSED sign in the window, retrieved the book from the hiding place, and sat down with the book on the front counter before him. He opened the cover and began to read.

10
The Outside People

It was midnight when Robert closed the book. It was like reading a fantasy children's story, a fairy tale. The difference being, the fairy tale was the real thing (or so a talking cat said). And he, Robert, had been chosen to read the "fairy tale" to find clues to return the said talking cat to the kingdom of Grindle to claim his throne. Robert laid his head down on the counter and shut his eyes. He could never talk about this to anyone; Katie would have him locked up if he told her.

Willie came running down the stairs and leaped up onto the counter.

"Well, Robert, tell me how I can go back to Grindle!" he asked, stamping his kitty feet on the counter with excitement.

Robert rolled his eyes and said, "Willie, who are these Outside People you speak of, the ones who are mentioned in the book?"

"You sure roll your eyes a lot, Robert. Do they bother you? Our Kingdom physician can whip up stuff to help that. Anyway, they are fairies that work on the outside. They look like ordinary people, but they have magical powers. They've been all around you, but you were not aware of them. They were in New York and one of them even delivered Mr. Redding's letter to you, the one instructing you to see him." Grooming his fur and purring, Willie curled his tail around his feet and continued. "They always stay on the outside as contacts in case they are needed in emergency situations."

"Don't they know how to return to Grindle?" Robert asked.

"Oh, they did once, but all the older ones died off and the new ones who were sent to replace them, were never told how and they don't know how to read either, so they just stay on the outside as helpers," Willie advised. "I'm getting hungry; anything good to eat out in the back room?"

Robert shook his head, got up and walked to the back. "I don't really know what to look for. That book tells the story of Grindle, the Moon flowers, wizardry, traditions, etc. As for the fairy ring, it mentions a certain three-quarter moon, full moon and a light beam and things that fit into other things, but doesn't ever come right out and say *what.* At least nothing that I can understand, so I'm going to need your help, Willie." He opened a can of cat food and emptied some into the cat's bowl, along with fresh water.

"If you read it to me, Robert, maybe I can fit the pieces together since I understand this fairy stuff and you don't. Just let me eat and then we will both give some thought to what it tells us."

11
The Fairy Ring

Robert sat at the table near the front counter and Willie curled up on top of it near him, as he began to read.

"This is basically what I think the book is saying. The night of the three-quarter moon will fall on the 7th of this month. And the full moon on the 17th. A moonbeam will shine on the first stone of the Fairy Ring, whatever that is, on those days. It will last for four seconds on the 7th, and on the 17th, the moonbeam will hold its position for four minutes. The seventh stone from the first, will hold the key to the entry to Grindle. But which way do you count to the seventh stone from the first one? And you will have to be quick or the moonbeam will move and fall on the wrong stone. Then one stone fits into another and good grief, Willie, how do they ever expect anybody to find out anything? They certainly don't make it easy."

"I know what," offered Willie. "Why don't you rent a car and let's take a drive to the fairy ring and see what the situation looks like?"

Robert thought to himself, of course; just rent a car and go find a fairy ring! Maybe someday he would tell Sam. Sam would probably be the only one who would not question Robert's sanity because he was a little insane himself. Katie was another story. She would try to find him some professional help.

The next day, he and Willie took a cab to the car rental agency, where he picked a small economical one. He put Willie on the seat next to him and off they went. Willie got up on his hind feet with his front paws on the dashboard. As he looked out the windshield, his eyes widened and he jumped up, hiding his head in the back of the seat and hollered, "YOU'RE DRIVING ON THE WRONG SIDE OF THE ROAD!"

"Don't yell, I've got enough problems sitting on the right side of the car, shifting on the left. Maybe when we get out into the country, it won't be so bad."

Willie finally lifted his head and peeked over the door through the window and sighed. Robert was managing to stay on the proper side of the road. After driving around the "Round About" a few times, he finally made his way onto the road Willie told him to take. Making their way to the highway, with Willie's navigation, things smoothed out a bit.

"How far is this place we're going to, Willie?" Robert asked.

"I don't know. It's been a long time since I was there. But if you stay on this road, you will come to a fork in the road. One side goes to Trowbridge, the one we want. When we get there, wake me up, it's nap time." Willie lay down and wrapped his paws over his nose and fell fast asleep. Robert wondered how he could do that so quickly. He also wondered how Willie knew that this was the right road, but he was learning fast that it did no good to question, he would just have to do as he was told.

After a couple hours, Robert shook Willie. "Okay, we're at the fork in the road. One goes to Wiltshire and the one we want goes to Trowbridge." The sleepy cat stood up, stretched, yawned and looked out the windshield. As they drove on, large stones began to appear on the horizon. Robert saw a sign pointing to the road to Stonehenge. He'd never seen it in person, only in pictures.

"Turn on this road, Robert."

As they got closer, the bigger and more massive the stones were. Robert was awe-struck by the sight. When they reached the structure, the road led into a parking area and ended.

"Okay, now what, Willie? The road ends here."

"We're here."

"This is Stonehenge, Willie," said Robert hesitantly, waiting for a response he was afraid would come and that he wouldn't believe.

"Yeah, and a real beauty, isn't it?" Willie stared at the structure and smiled. "It's been a long time. Looks like some of the stones have toppled over. Guess we'll have to fix that."

"Willie, this is Stonehenge," Robert repeated.

"Well, *we* don't call it Stonehenge, *we* call it the 'Fairy Ring,' " said Willie. "I know, all you guys and the scientists and archaeologists all are still trying to figure out what it is and what it means and how they were put together and all that stuff. Actually if they would just ask me, I could tell them and save them all that trouble."

Robert dropped his head, shut his eyes and thought maybe this was all a dream. "It can't be," he said to himself in a deflated voice. "It just *can't* be. For thousands of years, it's been a mystery and now along comes a talking cat that tells me it is a FAIRY RING?"

Willie stared at Robert for a while and finally said, "Well? Are we going to go check things out, or what?"

Robert, numb from the revelation, took the keys from the ignition and opened the car door. Willie bounded out, ran a short distance and stopped to wait for him. After a few minutes of walking, they stopped.

"Willie, maybe your fairy ring is nearby and you are mistaken about this," Robert said to the cat. He studied Willie's face hoping to see some sort of perplexity. But he did not and Willie showed excitement instead.

"Nope! This is it and it's just as magnificent as it was when I saw it as a child. I was here once before, you know, when the Moon flowers appeared and opened up releasing the new fairies. The moonbeam shines on them and all that stuff. Anyway, right now, we have to figure out the puzzle." Willie paced back and forth, swishing his tail. Robert stood looking at the huge boulders with a blank stare.

Finally, Robert said with a sigh. "There's a small fence around it, which will prevent me from getting close to it. But you're a cat and since cats are always lurking around places, you can check it out and then tonight after dark and the tourists have gone, we'll come back and investigate it more thoroughly."

"Okay, I'll be right back," replied Willie as he bounced over the rocks and slinked through the tall grass. Robert watched Willie, trying to imagine his kind of world, all the time thinking he was experiencing something here that he could not tell just anyone and still be respected as a sane person.

Willie nonchalantly sauntered up to one of the tall, massive boulders standing like a proud sentry, and rubbed against the base. He then disappeared around to the other side. He was out sight for a short period of time and then he reappeared. Standing around nearby, were a lot of tourists, young and old, talking among themselves and in tour groups. They were taking photographs, pointing and discussing what might have caused this unique and ominous structure and coming to their own conclusions. Robert stood there with an uncontrollably hysterical urge to yell out, "THIS THING WAS MADE BY A BUNCH OF FAIRIES!"

Willie soon came back slinking through the tall grass again and making an occasional leap for a grasshopper. He rubbed against Robert's leg and whispered.

"I think I've found the first stone! Come on, let's go." The two of them walked back to the car with Robert stopping a few times, turning and looking at what was known as Stonehenge. He just shook his head. Willie hopped around after butterflies and stopped to scratch his ear. They failed to notice the figure with bright red hair in the crowd, who turned to watch them as they left.

They found a Bed-and-Breakfast inn in the town of Trowbridge. Robert checked in and Willie slipped around to the back of the building to check out the other cats he'd seen upon arriving. Maybe they would know the source of some food. He was getting hungry. Later that evening after dinner in the small dining room of the inn, Robert went outside to find Willie, who was waiting on the hood of the car.

"Hurry, Robert, the moon is up. By the way, what day is this?"

"It's the 7th, Willie," he answered.

"What luck! Come on, let's go!" said Willie, jumping up and down with excitement.

The large stones stood dark against the night sky. Robert parked the car just outside the fenced area. The man and the cat got out and stealthily made their way to the fence. They found a spot that was shaded from the moonlight by a stone and Robert quickly climbed over. Willie followed and off they went to the large boulder that Willie suspected as being the one they needed, the first stone. Robert hoped no one would see him. He didn't know if the site was watched at night by Park Rangers or not. If he were caught, he could just see the headlines. "CRAZY AMERICAN CAUGHT SNEAKING INTO STONEHENGE MUMBLING SOMETHING ABOUT FAIRIES!"

Everything was very peaceful and serene. The moonlight was almost magical, as it seemed to dance and twinkle on the stones. Willie bounded ahead of him.

"Come on, Robert, we haven't much time. This stone over here has a crack through it from the top and I think it's the one we're looking for."

Robert stared at the stone, as Willie called it, and thought it had to be the size of a Greyhound bus standing on its end with another Greyhound bus lying crossways on top of it. The moon was in the sky behind it and cast a beam of light through the crack, reflecting at the bottom, creating what appeared to a pointer to the right. It was clear to Robert that this represented the line drawings in the book. The seventh stone would reveal the secret they hoped to find.

"See, Robert, this is it and the moonbeam is pointing over there! Come on, let's get to the seventh one." Just as he said that, the moonbeam began to move further down the stone. Willie ran past him and at the seventh stone, he ran around and around it.

"There's nothing here; it's just a big piece of granite with a real bad chip on this side!" he yelled.

"There is supposed to be another part to the puzzle, Willie. We'll have to go back to the shop and try to figure out what it might be. At least we have part of it solved."

"Well, we'll have to figure out the rest of it before the 17th, Robert, or the time of my return will be delayed," said Willie, impatiently.

They both made their way back to the fence keeping in the shadows. Again, Robert climbed over and back to the car they went. Willie sat down next to him, his eyes wide with anticipation. As the car sped down the road to Trowbridge, a cloaked figure stepped out from behind one of largest stones and disappeared into the night.

Neither of them slept much. Robert lay wide awake and noticed the shadow of Willie's tail as he jumped from the windowsill into the night.

What a great life a cat leads; he eats, sleeps and carouses at night. Not unlike some of the guys I work with, thought Robert.

The next morning, after a cup of coffee and a biscuit, Robert checked out of the inn. He went outside and found Willie perched on the hood of the car again.

"These country cats are more down to earth, you know," Willie explained. "Not as up-tight as the city cats. Okay, let's go. I want to get back, we have work to do."

Robert smiled and realized he was becoming quite accustomed to this talking cat and would miss him when this was all over.

12

The Search

When they returned to London, Robert dropped Willie off at the bookstore. He checked around to make certain everything was okay. He put food and water in the bowls for him.

"See you tomorrow, my friend. I'm going to take the book to my room and study it some more." Robert looked at a sleepy cat, who was getting ready to curl up for some nap time.

After Robert left, Willie slipped out through the small hole in the door for a quick visit to the sandbox, when a dark figure stepped out from behind a dumpster. Before Willie could run, a big bag swooped him up and flipped him upside down.

"I have you now, you stupid cat, or should I say, 'your highness.' " There was that awful cackly but gleeful voice of Hilga! Willie panicked and began to sound out big meows hoping she would mistake him for a regular cat. But she did not let him go!

Robert awoke the next morning and went to the window to open the shutters. On the window ledge was a note secured by a big hatpin.

"The final key is in your hands, William is in mine! If you want to see him again, you will give me the key!" the note read.

"Hilga!" Robert said, stunned. He was growing very fond of Willie and now he must act fast. Since he had no idea where to start, he decided to contact the Outside People. But how would he find them? Perhaps he would let them come to him, since they seemed to know everything that was happening, anyway.

He quickly showered and dressed, hoping someone from the Outside would contact him. Picking up the brass key, he felt the now familiar finger tingling as before. He looked carefully at it.

"What the . . . This isn't brass at all. IT'S GOLD! THE KEY TO THE PUZZLE!" It was so obvious, why hadn't he discovered it before now! He quickly slid the key into his pocket. Things were beginning to come together. But there was still the third piece yet to solve.

He put the OPEN sign in the front window of the bookstore and sat on the stool behind the counter. He wasn't sure what he was waiting for, but didn't know what else to do. Suddenly, standing before him was Hilga with that frowzy red hair under the same floppy hat. She just appeared out nowhere, with that stupid looking dog-like "thing." In that menacing voice, she said, "William is fine for now, but I will be back in four days for that book and the key so I can return to Grindle. If you don't come up with what I want, William will be on his way to a new adventure. You have work to do, so you'd better move quickly!" she hissed as she turned and vanished right through the door. Robert looked after her, watching an ugly lopsided creature running after her, making that awful noise. He just now realized she hadn't even opened the door. They both walked *through* it . . .

Robert quickly went up to the loft and to the loose board in the back wall. It glittered with the silver and gold dust and as he looked at it, he realized that it was not wood at all, but stone. It was a jagged piece of stone about a foot long and it blended right in with the rest of the wood. "That's why the nails kept flying out when I tried to hammer them into it," he whispered to himself. "This piece of stone looks like it is the chip from the seventh stone at Stonehenge. And this indentation is in the shape of the key! Why didn't I notice this before?" He slid his hand into the hollow behind the stone and pulled out the book. Opening it to the line markings, it showed exactly the same number and positions of the stones at the "Fairy Ring."

Robert put the book back behind the piece of stone and walked down the steps trying to think of what to do next, when the front door opened, to reveal Merlin.

"I understand you need my help," he offered.

Robert looked at him and asked, "Are you one of them?"

"Are you asking if I am an Outside person? If so, yes, I am. However, and more pertinent—word around the neighborhood is that Willie has disappeared. That old witch has him."

"Hilga! Yeah, she has Willie. She left me a note and then she came in, threatening that something awful will happen to Willie If I didn't give her what she wanted," Robert replied.

"I know. Sherlock told me. He was dining in the garbage can out back and saw the whole thing."

"Sherlock?"

"He's the cat Willie chummed around with. He taught Willie cat talk and Willie taught him people talk. Good thing too, because he was able to tell me what happened. He banded his group together and wants to help search, but first he wanted to assure you not to worry. He and a few of his and Willie's friends are waiting out back. Okay to come in?" asked Merlin.

"Of course," said Robert.

Merlin walked to the back door and opened it. In came a big black cat with big green eyes and a white spot on one ear.

"Sherlock reporting, sir!" said the cat, as he saluted with a paw over one eye.

"HUT, ONE, TWO, THREE, FOUR!" the cat yelled. Suddenly, the sound of small marching feet was heard and then in came cat after cat, marching in unison through the door. Big cats, little cats, cats with long tails, cats with short tails, orange cats, and yellow cats. Black cats, white cats, cats with spots and cats with stripes. On and on they came, hundreds of them all marching in close order. Robert thought he had never seen so many cats at one time in his life. They were everywhere, row after row downstairs, upstairs, and up and down the stair steps. And was that humming he heard? It was very faint, but sounded suspiciously like the theme from "Bridge on the River Kwai." Finally the last cat came in, marched into his place, and the humming stopped.

"I've gathered a few of us together to scour the city in search of our friend, Willie," announced Sherlock. "He can't be too far. Okay gang, let's go!" he ordered in a military tone.

What happened next was total chaos. The cats all scrambled and ran everywhere, running into each other, up and over bookshelves, leaping over tables causing Robert and Merlin to flatten themselves against the wall to avoid getting run over. An occasional altercation here and there, yowling and hissing, meowing, jumping over the counter—and finally, everyone out the front door.

"What was that?" exclaimed Robert.

“Oh, *that,*” said Sherlock, who was left standing in the middle of the floor. “They practiced and practiced marching into the book store, but they didn’t have time to practice marching OUT of the store.”

“We’ll find him,” assured Merlin as he followed Sherlock out the door.

Well, at least they didn’t walk through it, thought Robert.

13
Playing the Palace

That evening, Katie called and asked, "When are you coming back, Robert? You should have things pretty much taken care of there—or are you planning to stay?"

"I can't leave just yet, Katie," said Robert, lamely. "The cat has disappeared and I have to find him before I can leave."

"You've never even liked cats before this, so why are you trying to find a cat that's used to living in alleys? He was doing that when you got there, Robert." Katie was becoming quite irritated.

"I know, Katie, but this cat is kind of different. I just can't leave without knowing what's become of him. It shouldn't be too much longer now. I'll call you soon. Good-bye." He thought he'd better hang up quickly before she could ask any more intimidating questions.

He hadn't heard from Merlin or the cats for a while, and was growing quite concerned. On the fourth morning he opened the store for business as usual. He kept himself busy, while at the same time worrying about Willie. As Robert stepped out from behind a bookshelf, there stood Hilga. She was such a sight, almost comical with those black wingtips hanging behind her. And that "thing" that followed her around. It didn't have any fur to speak of, it was bald and gray.

"Well?" Hilga smirked menacingly.

Robert calmly advised her, "I am sorry madam, I don't know what you are after. I know nothing about a key to anything."

This infuriated Hilga. She stomped her foot and screeched.

"You'll be sorry and so will that cat!" She disappeared, this time, right before Robert's eyes. Shutting his eyes, he shook his head in disbelief. When he opened them, there stood the disreputable "creature." Then all of a sudden, with a yelp, *poof,* it too vanished.

Two more days went by and no further word about Willie. When evening came, Robert hung the CLOSED sign on the front door. He went to the back to put fresh food and water into Willie's bowls, as he had been doing since he disappeared, hoping the cat would come back and would want food.

Robert heard a small scratching on the back door. He listened again, not sure of what he heard. There it was again, so Robert quickly flung open the door. Down at his feet was a large blob of white-looking stuff, and out of the end were those big yellow eyes blinking at him. Robert stared at the blob as it clomped into the shop.

"Willie? Is that you?"

"I'm starved, Robert! What's for dinner?" Robert reached down to touch him and felt a hardening doughy gunk sticking all over him.

"Where have you been, Willie? And how did you escape from Hilga! And what is this horrible stuff all over you?"

"Well, it's like this, you see . . . *Ppppffffit!"* He sputtered. "The day we came home, I went outside to do personal stuff, you know, and all of a sudden a big black bag swooped me up and I couldn't get out! I heard our friend

Hilga's voice snickering something about how she had me now. Then I was put into a cage for a few days. I couldn't tell where I was, but it seemed like some sort of warehouse. I was given some water and a few small morsels to eat. Then one day Hilga came in with a nicely dressed man. They exchanged some words in the other room. I couldn't hear what they were saying, but apparently they came to some sort of agreement. He then walked into the back room and picked up my cage and we left. We soon came to a tall iron gate and the man pushed a button. Pretty soon another man came out wearing a tall furry hat and a red suit. He clicked his heels a lot. Anyway, he opened the big iron gate and let us inside. We walked through another large door and entered a beautiful big garden. Next to the garden was another door leading into a big kitchen where people were wearing white coats and tall white hats and aprons and running all around. They stopped when we entered and looked at me. Then they went around and around the cage I was in and said I looked okay, but I would have to be examined by the palace vet.

"Now, let me tell you, Robert, that was an experience! Have you ever had anybody stick fingers in your ears and mouth and other places? I was then taken back to the kitchen and let out of the cage. The man then told the kitchen people that I was the 'Royal Mouser.' Can you believe that? They wouldn't feed me anymore, because I was supposed to dine on royal mice! Then at night when the cooking and cleaning was done in the kitchen, they put me in the wine cellar where I had to stay for the night. It was a good thing there were plenty of livestock there, or I would have starved!

"Then one evening a couple days later, a big fancy dress dinner was taking place in the royal dining room. A lot of scurrying and hustling was going on in the kitchen when a large commotion was heard outside the door that led to the garden. A lot of yowling and carrying on, so the cook opened it to see what was going on and one of my cat friends, Horton, landed smack on his head! While the cook was wrestling with Horton, the rest of the gang, and even some cats I didn't know, came running into the kitchen with Sherlock leading them. The other cooks were chasing them, hollering, and yelling, and waving wooden spoons in the air. The servers and the maids who came into the kitchen from the dining room carrying trays of dishes and stuff, were tripped by the cat swarm! Everything flew into the air when they fell, causing the floor to get slippery from the sauces and soups, which made it a little difficult standing up. They were sliding all around, grabbing table legs or anything to pull themselves up. In the meantime, Sherlock and I were going to make a quick getaway, but the head cook slammed the door shut, that had been left open. He had been told by the nicely dressed man who took me there, who was told by Hilga, that if they let me get away, it would be the royal sewer rooter job for him! He grabbed me and was going to throw me into the wine cellar, but I wriggled and escaped his clutches, only to fall into the cake batter.

"Have you ever tried to get out of a bowl of cake batter, Robert? Boy, you just slide all over! Anyway, I finally got a grip on the bowl and threw myself over the side. The cook made a grab for me but I slid right out of his hands. I finally made it through the door into the dining room just in time to see the senior cat Frank, sitting right on top of one of the roast ducks in the middle of the table. Ebinezer was pulling his feet out of the mashed potatoes, and Petunia had landed on the plate of a woman wearing a sparkly hat and carrying a small purse on her arm. Then ole Jake, who after jumping from the food server at the side of the table, landed square into the gravy boat, splattering gravy everywhere, dripping off the ladies' hairdos. All of the people at the table were in such a state, squealing and carrying on, you'd think they'd never seen a couple hundred cats before!

"Anyway, everyone was up, running, chasing and yelling and the humans were throwing things! During all of the racket, we managed to go from the dining room back into the kitchen and out the back door that had been opened by one of the maids who ran out screaming.

"A bunch of us hid in the garden until dark so we could make our escape over the wall. We could hear some men searching, and one was saying something about how he didn't want to work in the sewer. Finally when it became dark, the men decided we'd all gone, so they gave up and went inside. We then climbed the old oak tree and jumped to the other side of the wall. And here I am!"

Robert stared at the cat, thinking this was the funniest sight he'd seen in a long time. He was so overjoyed to see Willie, but he couldn't muffle a smile and then hysterical laughter.

"What are you laughing at? I could've been stuck in that wine cellar eating royal mice for the rest of my life!"

14
The Return

After a soaking in warm soap and water, Robert washed all of the flour and water mixture out of Willie's fur. He rinsed him well and toweled him off. Willie groomed himself the rest of the way and soon he looked like a cat again.

"I have discovered the final key to the puzzle, Willie. The piece of stone that was missing from the boulder, was the piece protecting the book in the wall; and this brass key isn't brass at all, but gold—and it is the KEY that ignites the process of the transfer. We have it, Willie!"

Willie, exhausted from his adventure, smiled.

"I knew you would do it, Robert. You are truly my friend and that's why I want you to see my Kingdom. I wouldn't take just anybody, you know. Now, I'm really tired and would just like to have a good night's sleep." He sauntered to the blanket that was provided for him on the floor and curled up with his tail wrapped around his head and was soon fast asleep. Robert watched him for a few minutes, then got up to leave after saying goodnight to Willie.

The next day, Robert went to the loft in the bookstore. He carefully lifted the book, *The Seventh Stone,* from its hiding place and put it on the table. He then took his hammer and with the claw foot, pried the stone from the spot where it was wedged. He placed both the stone and the book into a cloth bag and went downstairs.

Willie was waiting at the bottom for him.

"Let's go, Robert, before that Hilga comes back! I have to get to Grindle. Tonight is the 17th and this is my last chance or I will have to wait another whole year!"

Robert took the gold key from his pocket and when they left the shop, he turned the key in the lock for, what he did not know, was to be the last time.

Again, they took a cab to the car rental agency. Once in the car, excitement became apparent in Willie, as did apprehension in Robert. Robert really wasn't too sure he was ready to leave a somewhat normal world, which didn't seem too normal lately, to travel to a land of "Fairies."

Finally, they came to the fork in the road, Wiltshire to the right and Trowbridge to the left. Taking the left of the fork, Robert could see in the distance the massive stones standing ominously against the sky. It was around 1:30 P.M. and they had the afternoon to plan their strategy. Willie was standing on his hind legs with his front paws placed on the dashboard licking his chops nervously, knowing by tomorrow, with luck, he would be home.

Robert packed some cheese, bread and bottled water, and some kitty snacks for Willie. That way, they would not have to leave for Wiltshire for lunch and risk having something happen that would prevent them from returning. The day passed by slowly as Robert and Willie sat on the grassy hill near the fenced area. They'd eaten the snacks and were now waiting for night to come and the tourists to leave the park.

"We will have four minutes to make the transport, Robert. You will have to hang onto my hand, or paw, for us to go through together. Then when you are ready to come back, we will transport you back here or wherever you would like to be. But you just have to see Grindle and the fairies! And during the transport, I will be changed back into William, and not to brag or anything, I really have a great set of WINGS! In fact, I'm rather quite handsome. What's the matter, Robert?" asked Willie as he stood up on Robert's lap looking him in the eyes. "It's the wing thing, isn't it?"

Evening finally came and the tourists began to leave. The great Ring of Stones stood alone in the darkness like a safe-keeper of history.

"Okay, Willie, let's go. I have the piece of stone and the key. I just hope this works."

"You're going to love it Robert, it really is beautiful! And you will be just in time to witness the new fairies emerging from the Moon Flowers. They bloom only at night, and only on this date, when the moonbeams shine on them. The little fairies unfold the Moon Flower petals and Voilà!"

New fairies popping out of flowers? thought Robert. *I will always have a hard time believing this.*

Robert climbed over the fence and Willie followed.

"The moon is shining on the first stone," said Robert. "In a minute the moonbeam will be shining though the crack, then we will have four minutes to go to the seventh one and fit the chipped piece of stone into the large one. Then when the key is placed in the indentation, we'll be on our way. Are you ready, Willie?"

When the moonbeam shined through the crack down to the dent showing them which direction to follow, Robert and Willie ran counting the stones to the seventh one and quickly placed the stone chip into its place. Robert took the gold key from the bag and placed it into the indentation and waited for what seemed like forever for something—he didn't know what.

Suddenly everything was calm and still. There was an eerie feeling, as a breeze passed Robert's face like a feather. Then it turned into a violent wind that gradually spawned a funnel. Robert felt himself being lifted off the ground. Willie was spinning in the air. Suddenly they heard Hilga behind them. She grabbed Willie, but could not hold on and was spinning uncontrollably. Willie felt his powers coming back and just as Hilga again tried to reach for him, he raised his paw and pointing at her, spoke a few fairy words and she dropped onto the grass below.

"OH, DARN!" she sputtered, as she disappeared into a big "Poof!" Gargoyle, still standing with wide eyes and showing big teeth, was next with a big "Poof!" There he went.

"My powers are back, Robert!" Willie excitedly exclaimed. Robert reached for Willie's paw, but was yanked away by a strong gust. He heard Willie yell at him as he started fading out of sight.

"We have lost contact, Robert, but I've left you something that will help you come to Grindle another time. Call it a 'gift.' Good-bye until next time!"

Amazed, Robert stared at the swirling wind as the handsome future King of Grindle with his magnificent wings gradually disappeared before him.

The wind threw Robert to the ground with a thud. The winds were gone and all that was left was the fog and mist. In an instant, it was quiet, as before; so still he could hear his own heart beat. Then the fog was gone and the moon and stars in a brief moment began to glitter and dance in the sky.

Willie is home, where he should be, thought Robert.

He sat on the grass for hours trying to comprehend everything from his first day in London until tonight when he lost a friend to—would you believe—a "land of the fairies."

He got up, walked back to the rental car and turned to look at majestic Stonehenge . . . "Okay, Fairy Ring." He looked to the heavens and said, "Maybe I will go to Grindle someday!"

15

Bag of Sand

It was almost a year since Robert returned from his trip to London. He tried to return to a normal lifestyle, but the past events were constantly in his thoughts. He had been promoted assistant to the assistant of the head accountant in the Motley Accounting Firm. He referred to himself and the other two as "The Motley Crew."

Katie and Sam still worked at the museum and the three of them continued their get-togethers at the local café to hash over the day's events. They questioned Robert at first about the bookstore he left behind in London and what he did in the weeks that he spent there, but he seemed to not want to discuss anything, so they eventually dropped the subject. Once Sam asked him if he'd had a chance to get away and see Stonehenge, only to have Robert choke on his sandwich. He never answered the question.

One day after work, Katie was in Robert's apartment, waiting for him to change into some casual clothing before going out to dinner. She was looking at his collection of books in the shelves, when she found a small leather bag tied with a leather strap. She didn't know whether to look inside or not. It felt as though it was filled with sand, but had a sort of movement to it.

"What's in this little leather bag, Robert—sand?" she

yelled to him. But there was no answer. She cautiously untied the leather strap, pulled open the gathered top and peeked inside. It looked like sand, but it had a sparkle to it. She then tilted the bag and poured some of the contents out onto the end table near the couch. She stared at what appeared to be silver and gold dust. She reached down with her fingers to touch the small mound of granules, when Robert came out of the bedroom and exclaimed to her, “Katie, don’t!”

Startled, Katie jumped, hitting the table and dumped half of the dust onto the floor, with most of it settling into the fibers of the carpet.

“Robert, I’m so sorry, I thought it was just a bag of sand! I’ll clean it up with the Dust Buster. By the way, it looked as though it was glowing, but I guess it was just the sun shining through the window.”

“Don’t worry about it, Katie, I’ll clean it up later,” Robert replied.

“What is it, Robert? The stuff felt funny when I held the bag. It sort of moved in my hand.”

“Oh, just an experiment Sam and I are working on. Come on, let’s go, if we want to make our reservations.” Not being prepared for the question, he didn’t want to have to come up with an explanation.

The next day at the museum, Katie asked Sam about the experiment he and Robert were working on.

“What experiment?” asked Sam.

“The one with the silvery-gold, sandy stuff, that Robert keeps in a little leather bag in his apartment. He got very nervous when he saw me accidentally pour it onto the table. In fact, he startled me and I knocked some of it on the carpet.”

"I don't know anything about an experiment with any sand," said Sam.

"It had a glow to it, and I swear the stuff moved in the bag when I held it. . . . Oh, well, let's get to work and talk about it later."

"What's this about some kind of sand experiment, Robert? Katie told me you and I were working on an experiment?"

"Sam, I want to talk to both you and Katie. It has to do with the sand, as you call it. Tell Katie, and the two of you come on over after work. Can't talk now." Robert hung up the phone and tried to concentrate on the pile of work he had sitting on his desk.

About six o'clock, Sam and Katie showed up at Robert's apartment. Robert poured glasses of iced tea and the three of them sat down in the living room.

"You look very mysterious, Robert," observed Katie.

"Yeah, and quite frankly, you haven't been quite the same since you came back from England. What's bothering you, Robert?" asked Sam.

"Okay, here goes. You're not going to believe me. I tried to avoid saying anything because you'll both think I'm crazy." Robert cleared his throat and began from the beginning, describing in detail the weeks he spent in London. From Solicitor Redding, to Merlin, to Willie, to Hilga, to Gargoyle, and on and on.

As Robert talked, Katie and Sam sat staring at him, occasionally glancing at each other and back to Robert. Before he got to the part about Stonehenge and the Fairy Ring, Sam stood up from the chair and walked around the room.

"Fairies, huh? I've got to go." Sam headed for the door.

"No, don't go, Sam. I was telling the truth. I thought you, of all people, would believe me!"

"I take offense at that!" Sam shot back. "I may have different views on some things, but why would you think I would believe in fairies!"

"I meant no offense, Sam. But why would I make up a story like that?"

"I don't know, Robert," said Katie. "But I'd like to know what you really did in London. Was there really an inheritance, or a bookstore, or anything real about your time spent there?"

"The dust—maybe you'll believe the dust." He took the small leather bag from the shelf and poured the contents onto the table. The grains of the dust began to twinkle and move around. They began to form bits of words, as they moved. Sam came back from the door and Katie got up from the couch and moved closer. They both stared at the moving words that now began to form a sentence. "THE TIME IS NEAR—FROM THE SHOP IT'S A SHORT WALK TO SEE SH . . ."

"Quick, get the Dust Buster! We've got to get the rest of the dust up from the carpet to finish the sentence."

"You mean you haven't cleaned it up since the other day when I spilled it?" frowned Katie.

"Hurry!" shouted Robert. Katie and Sam just stood staring at each other.

"NOW!" Robert demanded. Both Katie and Sam ran to the closet, bumping into each other. Sam handed Robert the vacuum and backed away. Katie showed Robert the spot where she thought she'd spilled it.

As he worked, Katie said, "What's wrong with him, Sam? He's been so weird since London, I hardly know him anymore!"

"He has seemed preoccupied lately," answered Sam.

"I think he's been working too hard." As he spoke, Robert emptied the vacuum tank on the table and sifted through the contents to separate the one type of dust from another. He hoped he had enough to finish the words that appeared to be forming on the table, but because of the mixture of dust, it did not have enough energy to complete it.

"I'm going back," Robert said, calmly.

"Back? To what?" asked Katie. "You said you sold the bookstore, or rather that it had *disappeared,* as the story changed."

"I just have to go back! Come with me, both of you. Maybe I can convince you and hopefully myself, that I'm not crazy."

"What about it, Katie?" asked Sam. "We both have time coming from the museum and I think I want to go."

"Come on, Sam, it's got to be a trick, probably with a magnet or something, moving that stuff around. He's just playing with your mind," Katie argued.

"You can't form words like that with a magnet, Katie. I'm intrigued by this whole thing."

"You believe him?"

"I didn't say that. I just think it's time I had a vacation, that's all."

"Well, you know I can't just stay here wondering what you are doing in London. Guess I'll have to go too, to keep an eye on both of you." Katie turned to Robert and said, "Okay, we'll go with you, Robert. When do we leave?"

16
The Bookstore

On the train, traveling from Heathrow into London, Katie watched the countryside whiz by, while a million thoughts went through her head. Sam sat with his head tilted back, appearing to be asleep. He was actually wondering why Robert would think he would believe in fairies. And Robert focused on Katie, knowing she didn't believe him, and hoping the bookstore would appear again. Then she would know.

"There's a small hotel near the Thames called Greenpark. That's where we'll be staying. It's not far from the spot where the bookstore was on Pickwick Street." Katie nodded her head and smiled. *In a patronizing way*, Robert thought.

They caught a cab at the station and gave the driver the name of the hotel. He did not look familiar, or recognize him as Robert had hoped he would. When they arrived, they went to their rooms and unpacked. They met in the lobby to plan the day.

"Well, this hotel certainly isn't a five-star. Wonder if it has any stars at all," said Katie dolefully.

"How about a 'minus two' star," snickered Sam, as he and Katie giggled.

"I wanted to get close to the bookstore, if you two

don't mind," Robert said impatiently. "And that's where we're going now. It's not far, just a few blocks."

He started walking at a rather fast pace and Sam and Katie had to half run to keep up with him. As they reached Pickwick Street, Robert turned the corner cautiously, not knowing what to expect. As he walked further on, there stood the old warehouse with the broken window. He stood looking at it, while Katie and Sam watched from the corner.

"Maybe we're on the wrong street," suggested Sam. "You know, I am really thirsty. Look, there's a pub down there on the corner, let's go and get something to drink. It's been a long flight and we are kinda tired." He nudged Katie.

"Yeah, yeah, me too, and . . . does that sound okay, Robert?"

"Okay, sure. I am a little foggy from jet lag. That's a nice pub, by the way. I ate there once in a while when I was here." As they walked, he kept looking back at the old warehouse, hoping to see the bookstore that wasn't there.

They each had a cold drink and a sandwich. They visited with the bartender, who said he was glad to see Robert again. At least, he felt that was one thing they would believe about his story. When they were through and ready, they went outside and looked up and down the street deciding which way to go.

"Wait a minute," Katie said, squinting at something that seemed to be appearing before her eyes. She began walking back toward the old warehouse that wasn't an old warehouse anymore. There in its place, was an old sign swinging on black wrought iron hinges. "The Tower Shop," it read. Beneath the sign was the big old wooden door with heavy bolted hinges and the windows were of leaded panes, as Robert had described. It was there, after all.

Katie and Sam stared at the store front while Robert smiled.

"There it is! I knew it! We were just a little early, that's all."

"Are we on the right street?" asked Katie. "Maybe we crossed over another one and didn't pay any attention."

"Give up, Katie," said Sam. "You and I both know this is the same street. The old warehouse was here, and it has turned into Robert's bookstore. As weird as this is, I'm intrigued by the whole thing and I want to go inside. Come on, Robert, wipe that silly grin off your face. You were right, at least about this one."

The old door creaked when they opened it. Robert went in first feeling nostalgic at the sight of the familiar surroundings. Katie and Sam entered slowly, noticing the antiquated decor, the old fashioned fixtures and furniture. They kept bumping into each other as they walked around, sticking close together.

"It's spooky in here," whispered Katie, as she waved her hand across her face. "Something keeps fluttering at me."

Robert stood in the middle of the room, turned around and said, "Isn't it wonderful? They brought it back for me!"

At that moment, a voice from the back room said, "I'll be right there, Robert."

"Who is that? And how'd he know it's you?" asked Sam.

"They just do."

"They?" asked Katie.

"The Outside People."

"Oh, yeah, the Outside People, who are really fairies,

but when they're on the outside they have to look like real peo . . ."

Robert frowned at Katie, so she abruptly stopped talking.

"Hello, Robert!" said the old man as he shuffled from the back room. "Good to see you again." There was old Merlin. "I've been looking after the store for you since you left. Been about a year now. I got word you'd be coming back to make the transport. And who are these fine people?"

"Merlin, I'm so relieved to see you and the bookstore again! This is Katie and Sam. Actually they just came along to keep an eye on me, they think I've been working too hard."

"Make yourself at home. I'll make some tea in the back. Then you must tell me what you've been doing this past year!"

Robert watched as he went into the back room. Same hunched-over Merlin, with those long feet.

Katie and Sam wandered about the store. Katie scanned the books in the shelves and as she reached out to touch one, she heard a tinkling sound along with feeling a tingling sensation from the book.

"I think that Merlin man is just as weird acting as Robert," whispered Sam to Katie, as she jerked her hand away from the books. She moved along to the other side of the bookshelves. She brushed what seemed like a feather from her face.

"What keeps fluttering past my face, Sam?" she exclaimed.

They each accepted a cup of tea and sat at the large table behind the railing. Katie kept milling about the store, nervously drinking her tea, while Sam enjoyed the conversation held by Merlin and Robert. Finally, an unseen presence spooked Katie and she announced that she would wait outside for them.

"I felt funny in there, didn't you, Sam?" asked Katie as they left the bookstore ahead of Robert.

"Yeah, I guess, but in a kind of magical peaceful way."

"Not you too, Sam! Not only that, but that old man said he'd been watching the bookstore for Robert. How could he, when it wasn't there in the first place?"

Sam just shrugged.

"So, where to next?" asked Sam, as Robert closed the heavy wooden door, bidding good-bye to Merlin.

"I'm not really sure. I'll have to try to figure out who the dust wanted me to find. The person can't be far, because it said a short walk from the store. But which direction? And will I know when I get there?"

"Well, I don't know where you two are going, but the dust told me to go back to the hotel and take a long hot bath and go to bed. I'm beat!" snickered Katie, as she waved good-bye and walked toward the hotel.

"Don't be sarcastic!" hollered Robert.

"You know, this is pretty unbelievable stuff, Rob," said Sam.

"I know, I thought I'd lost my mind when all of this started happening to me! Can you imagine being approached by a talking cat?"

Sam glanced at him out of the corner of his eyes.

"Come on, let's us call it a day, too." Robert continued, "Maybe tomorrow, things will appear more in perspective."

I have a feeling nothing will ever be in perspective again from this day forward, thought Sam.

17
Here Kitty, Kitty

The next morning, Katie was up early, feeling good after a long night's sleep. She decided to go out and do some exploring before meeting the guys for breakfast. She slipped a note under Robert's door saying she would be back in an hour and would meet him and Sam in the hotel lobby.

She walked a few blocks, turning corners and down side streets. She windowshopped and enjoyed the crisp morning air. She crossed an entrance to an alley when she heard a sort of tinkling sound, reminding her of small wind chimes, the same as in the bookstore. Then . . .

"Pssst."

She stopped and listened.

"Pssst."

There it was again. She looked around her and toward the alley. There was nothing there, except for a cat sitting next to the building. She walked over to the cat and as she reached down to pet it, the cat smiled and said, "I'm Sherlock."

Katie jerked her hand away and stepped back away from the cat. And when she looked around to see if anyone was there, no one was. When she looked back, the cat was gone.

"Okay, now I'm beginning to see and hear things like Robert," she said aloud. She quickly walked away from the alley, crossing the street into an area of small, quaint shops. Among them was a china shop with beautiful china pieces in the windows. She decided she would come back when the store was open and check it out. As she turned to head back to her hotel, she heard that same tinkling chime sound. She looked back at the shop noticing an odd looking gargoyle perched above the door. It seemed to have a duck-like foot on one side. She shuddered and briskly walked back to the hotel.

Robert and Sam were waiting for her in the lobby.

"Where have you been?" asked Robert. "Things don't open till nine here!"

"I took an early morning walk and now I'm very hungry. Let's eat," she said.

As they ate, Katie seemed nervous and just sat picking at her food.

"What's wrong, I thought you said you were hungry?" queried Robert.

"I feel silly, even saying this, but something happened when I was out this morning . . . no, it's nothing, forget it."

"Are you okay? What happened?" insisted Robert.

"It really is silly, I probably just imagined it. But I was walking along some side streets and there was this cat sitting in an alley and when I reached down to pet it, it looked like it smiled at me. Then . . . it . . . *spoke.*" She whispered, waiting for both Robert and Sam's reaction.

"It *what?*" asked Sam.

"It spoke to me," Katie repeated.

"Katie, think very carefully, what did the cat say?" asked Robert.

"What did the cat say?" snickered Sam, peering intently at Robert.

"It said, 'I'm Sherlock'," she replied.

Robert jumped up, spilling his coffee and quite loudly

said, "Sherlock! That's it! Just a short walk, see Sherlock! That's it!"

"Calm down, people are looking at us!" whispered Sam.

"Katie, where did you see the cat? What did he look like and where did he go?" Robert excitedly asked.

"Not too far from here," she explained. "I don't remember which street it was on. All I can remember is that I turned a few corners and came to an alley. The cat was all black with a white spot on one ear, but I don't know where it went after that, because I sort of wanted to get away from it. Then I walked further down the street and then came to this china shop, which by the way has some exquisite china. I'd like to go back and get some."

Robert was looking at her impatiently. "What about Sherlock?"

"Anyway," she frowned at Robert, "something told me to turn around. You know, I keep hearing these chime-like sounds. So I looked up to the top of the door where there was this ugly carved creature. And it had a weird duck-like foot!"

"Gargoyle! I wonder what happened to Hilga! I can't believe things are coming together this fast." Robert smiled and sat back in his chair.

"We've got a lot of work to do. We have to find Sherlock again. He's got the answers."

Katie looked at Sam and said, "I really did hear that cat talk, Sam. I really *did!*"

"I don't think I'm too hungry anymore, either," said Sam. "Okay, let's go, I just have to see this!"

They paid for their breakfast and left the hotel.

"Which way did you go from here, Katie?"

"I turned right and walked a couple blocks that way, then, I think left, into a side street. It was kind of small and narrow, with alleyways, and that's where I saw the cat. Then, I think onto a street with a lot of shops. The china shop was there," explained Katie.

Robert looked at her with doubt. "You don't sound too certain of the directions you took. Let's just start and figure it out as we go along."

As they walked, Katie became more sure of the route she had taken. Then as they turned the corner onto the narrow street, she stopped.

"There's the alley!" she exclaimed.

Robert and Sam approached the alley, while Katie stayed where she was. But nothing was there. Then suddenly a big black cat with a white spot on its ear appeared out of nowhere.

"Sherlock! Am I glad to see you! This is Sam, and you've already met Katie," Robert said as he motioned for her to come closer. A couple of people were passing them on the sidewalk, so Sherlock waited till they had gone before speaking.

"Grizzard had Willie locked up in the castle tower! He's been there since he went back. The gold key is the only means of unlocking the door, but Grizzard zapped it back here and it ended up in the hands of Hilga, who hid it somewhere until she could figure out how to return to Grindle. She still wants to be the Wizard! Anyway, she is spending her time in a little china shop down the street. She even hung poor Gargoyle on a nail up over the door to the shop. If he should move, he would fall off and smash to pieces. Anyway, you need to find that key and get back to Grindle to rescue Willie!" Sherlock took a deep breath and waited for a response.

Katie and Sam stood there staring in awe at the cat.

"It really can talk—and quite well, too," noted Sam.

Robert turned to Katie and said, "Where is the china shop?"

18
The China Caper

Hilga had just opened the shop and was dusting off the fine chinaware and porcelain statuettes on the glass shelves. She handled the delicate pieces with care and admiration. She'd always had an expensive and exquisite taste and was quite delighted when this particular shop became available to her, by the planned and temporary disposition of the owner.

As she twirled around the room dusting and arranging, she sang:

"Ooooohhhhhhhh, I want to be Wizard of Grindle
Wizard I want to be. And when I find the heck
How to get back, I'll give the title to meeeeeeee.

"Oooooooohhhhhhhh, The toads and lizards will all
disagree, cause part of my stew they won't want to be.

"But the birds and the butterflies will all say Aye,
Because they have wings and so do I.
Ooooohhhhhhh, I want to be Wiz . . ."

"Stop that confounded screeching, you old witch!" hollered the gargoyle from just outside the door. "You're giving me a headache!"

"Oh, shut yourself up! How can you have a headache when you have nothing in it to ache!" Hilga hollered back with a snicker.

"There's some people coming, so quiet down so you don't scare them away!" the gargoyle hollered back.

"Some people?" Hilga smoothed her dress and ran her hand through her bright red hair, took a quick look at herself in the mirror, then dashed behind the door to the storeroom and peeked out. As the three of them walked inside the shop, Hilga's eyes widened.

"Well, well, if it isn't that Robert!" *How did he get back here and how did he know where to find me?* she thought.

"Oh look at these pieces, Robert!" Katie said as she went around the room lightly touching the delicate porcelain. "The figurines are exquisite and so life-like. Especially this Oriental one . . . it looks so real!" She reached out to the glass case and quickly pulled her hand back. She covered her mouth as her eyes widened. The Chinese figurine had blinked at her!

"Hello! Anybody here?" hollered Robert.

Hilga stepped from behind the door with a smile. "Welcome to my shop. What brings you back to London, Mr. Penny?" She stood there wearing that same dress, with that same sweater, covering those same black wings, but minus that floppy hat.

She looked better wearing the hat, thought Robert.

"I understand William is being held prisoner and that you have the key to the castle tower," stated Robert immediately. "I want the key, Hilga."

"Oh, but I don't have it, so I can't give it to you. Does that remind you of anything, Robert?" she responded.

"I know you either have it, or you know where it

is—and we intend to get it, Hilga. So please make it appear. Use your magical powers if you have to."

Hilga grew angry and began waving her hands in the air. "Leave this shop or I will turn all of you into toads!" she screamed.

"Well, I'm leaving," said Sam as he turned and ran toward the door.

"We'll be back!" Robert took Katie's hand and pulled her out of the shop.

"Did you see that figurine, Robert? It wasn't like the others, it, it . . ." Robert wasn't paying attention to what she was saying; he was totally intent on helping Willie, or rather William.

Sherlock was watching and listening just outside the door. He ran up to Robert and said, "I'll pull the troops together. They enjoyed the last caper so much, they're chomping at the bit for another one! We'll meet you here tonight at six. Hilga will be closing about that time and we'll find the key. It has to be there somewhere."

"Thanks, Sherlock." The three of them stood watching the cat disappear around the corner.

As they walked back to the hotel, none of them spoke. Robert was worried about William; Katie thinking it all had to be a dream, and Sam convinced this was much more exciting and interesting than working in a museum. They agreed to meet a little before 6:00 in the lobby.

The streets were almost empty, which seemed strange to Katie. Sam, walking at a lively pace, was anticipating what possibly could happen. Sherlock was in the alley alone, as they arrived. When he saw Robert, he stood straight up and saluted him. He then turned toward the alley and in his military tone hollered,

"HUT, HUT, ONE, TWO, THREE, FOUR!"

Out of the alley came cats. At least a hundred or so

cats, marching in rows with tails sticking straight up. Katie smiled at the sight of little marching kitty feet.

"There they go, they mean business! I can't wait to see them in action. I've never seen them at work, but I heard about it from Willie," said Robert, as he, Katie and Sam ran after the cat brigade. On they marched down the empty streets till they turned the corner onto the street where Hilga's shop was. Suddenly they all stopped and looked at Robert.

Sherlock said, "They are waiting for you."

Robert quietly turned the door handle and opened it. Hilga was setting a cup and saucer on the shelf, when she saw Robert and the crowd outside the door. She screamed and ran toward the back as they all stormed into the shop. Some of the cats jumped at Hilga, tripping her and knocking her to the floor, face down. Several other cats jumped on her and old Ralph sat on her head.

"Get these mangy cats off me!" Hilga screeched.

"Not yet, not till we find the key!" Robert yelled back.

The cats got started, jumping onto the shelves, looking behind and under the pieces of china. They began to remove the china by tossing cups and saucers into the air, while other cats caught the flying missiles and gently stacked them in order on the floor. Delicate cups, saucers, plates, cream pitchers, glasses and other items were sailing from one end of the shop to the other, all being plucked from the air and gently placed on other shelves. One yellow cat with a big fluffy tail caught the plates in its tail, sliding them down, up across its back and over its head into its paws, which then placed it on top of the other plates. The foragers would clean out one shelf and, if seeing no key, would go on to another. As they reached the shelves of delicate crystal, Hilga couldn't stand it any longer, watching her beautiful china being thrown from one end to the other.

"Okay! I'll tell you where the key is!" she yelled. "Tell them to stop!" Immediately the rummaging stopped and the shop became quiet. The cats sat down and patiently waited to hear about the hiding place.

"Get these mangy cats off me!" Hilga demanded.

"You are a witch, Hilga; remove them yourself!" Robert sneered as he paced around her.

"Oh, yeah," she said in a meek voice. Hilga zapped each cat to the other side of the room and sat up on the floor.

"I'll tell you where the key is on one condition, and that is, that I go back with you."

Robert stared at her.

"How do I know you will behave and not use your old tricks to harm us or Willie?"

"I want to be Wizard. Good wizards don't harm anyone," Hilga insisted. "And I know how to do wizard stuff and I will free Willie, I promise. Please, please, PLEASE take me with you!"

Sherlock trotted over to Robert, jumped up onto the counter near him and whispered into his ear.

"She really doesn't harm anyone, Robert. She just zaps them here and there. When she abducted Willie, she did send him to a good place where he would be taken care of. But look where he is now, at the hands of the mean Wizard Grizzard! He's locked in a tower with nothing but bread and water and any mice he can catch."

Robert turned to look at Sherlock. "Mice?"

"Yeah. Grizzard turned him back into Willie the cat and locked him up, after he returned."

Sam and Katie were still huddled in the corner,

where they took cover to escape the flying cups and saucers.

"She looks pretty harmless to me," said Sam.

"How about you, Katie?" asked Robert.

Hilga looked up at her with big sorrowful eyes, which Katie couldn't resist. "Oh, sure—let her go," Katie agreed.

All the cats jumped up and down and voiced approval, in cat cheers. Robert helped Hilga up from the floor and she brushed her rumpled clothes. Katie noticed Hilga's wings for the first time and stared with her mouth open.

19
The Key

"The key, Hilga! Where is the key?"

"I hid it in the Tower Shop, in a book."

"Which book?"

"Um, uh, well, I think I would recognize it if I saw it. I mean, that was a long time ago, for heaven's sake! I'm an old woman . . . but of course, not too old to be Wizard."

"Okay, Hilga, we are all going to the bookstore and look for that key. You'd better be on the level, or we won't take you back!" Robert motioned for everyone to follow as he grabbed Hilga by the arm and marched out the door.

"Wait just a dadburned minute!" demanded the gargoyle, who was hanging precariously on a single nail over the door. "Are you just going to let her leave the china shop without returning it to its rightful owner?"

Hilga looked up at Gargoyle with squinted eyes and glared at it.

"Hilga?" questioned Robert. "Do you know where the owner is?"

"Ooooh, alright," Hilga said as she stomped back into the store. "He's right over here." She approached the glass shelves and lifted out one figurine, placing it on the floor.

Katie's eyes got big and she poked Robert. "That's the one I thought looked weird and blinked at me! Oooh!"

Katie scrunched her face in a distasteful manner, as she watched Hilga.

"HOCUS POCUS, TWIGGLEY TWIG, WHIRL IT, TWIRL IT AND MAKE IT BIG!" The witch waved her arms in the air in circular motions. "POOF!" A big fat pig plopped onto the floor with a snort and an oink.

"WHOOPS!" exclaimed Hilga. She again made wild motions with her hands, mumbling some incantations. This time a huge, mean-looking bull with big horns appeared, looking quite bewildered.

"And she wants to be Wizard?" whispered Sam, who was again huddled in the corner with Katie, who in turn, reminded him of the proverbial "Bull in a China Shop."

"You know," said Hilga, wringing her hands, "I might just leave things as they are—without the bull, of course, you know—in case things don't quite work out in the Wizard department. I would be able to come back here and have the shop with all these pretty things." She looked around the room admiring the pieces.

"HILGA!" came the voice from the Gargoyle hanging outside.

"Oooooh, alright!" Hilga snarled back. By this time the bull was beginning to become annoyed and began stomping its feet and Robert could swear fire came from its nose.

"AWAY, AWAY WITH THIS MALE COW! BRING THE OWNER BACK AND NOW!" The bull went "Poof!" and in its place stood an Oriental man with a very quizzical look on his face.

"Can I help you folks find what you're looking for?" the Oriental man asked, staggering a little and feeling very confused, obviously not remembering what happened to him.

"We will be back another time, we have something to

do first," answered Robert. He took Hilga by the arm and led her out the door, with Sam and Katie close behind.

As they began walking down the street, they heard a loud "HEY!"

They looked back at Gargoyle and then at Hilga. "Are you just going to leave him there? He belongs in the castle—or rather, *on* it—and we also have to take him back with us."

"But he's such a pain!" whined Hilga. Then, after a pause, "Oh, if you say so." She flicked her hands about and Gargoyle gently left the nail and softly sailed down into her arms. The creature even appeared to be smiling.

They all (including the cats), made their way back to the Tower Shop. When they entered, Hilga looked around at the hundreds of books stacked side by side in shelves and on the tables. Hilga went to where she thought she had hidden the key—but the books had been rearranged.

"I . . . I'm not sure where it is now. I think the book is gone." Hilga rushed from one shelf to another.

Merlin entered from the back room. "Robert, you're all here! Did you find what you were looking for? Oh, yeah, I guess you did," he said as he glanced at Hilga.

"She hid the key in one of the books, but she doesn't know which one. I guess this is going to take awhile. We're all going to have to start looking and fast, because we're running out of time."

Once more, all the cats began jumping up on shelves, tossing books in the air, into the paws of the other cats, who in turn, flipped the pages. When nothing was found, the books were thrown to the first group of cats, who carefully placed them back into the space they had been plucked from. Robert had never seen such an organized system, thinking his accounting firm could stand some lessons from these cats. He, Katie and Sam worked another bookcase, unsuccessfully.

"What was the name of the book, Hilga?" asked Merlin.

"I . . . think it had the work lock in the title. It did! I remember now that I chose that one so I would know where to find it again!"

Merlin took the inventory log book from beneath the counter, opened the pages and began to scan the list of books sold in the past year. He came upon the *Great Locks of Scotland, Under Lock and Key, Goldie Locks,* and *How to Pick Locks. "How to Pick Locks?"* he thought. He didn't remember that one. He named the titles he'd found to Hilga, and she looked at him with a blank stare. Everyone stopped working and looked at her with anticipation. Suddenly, her eyes widened and her face lit up like a light bulb.

"*Water Life!* That's it! A book for children!" she exclaimed.

"What does that have to do with locks?" asked Robert.

"Well, I figured waterlife had to do with the critters that live in the water such as the ocean and the lakes, and then I got to the bigger fish and thought of legendary monsters and voilà! *The Lock Ness Monster!* I knew it had the word 'lock' in it somewhere." She stood very pleased with herself as she looked around the room at Robert, Katie, Sam, Merlin and all those cats.

"Well? Do you have that book, Merlin?" asked Robert, as they all gathered around him. Merlin turned the pages to the "W's" and moved down the page with his finger.

"I sold it."

"You sold it?"

Merlin read further. "To a Mister Bellows, who

bought the book to give to his son for his birthday. It was sold three weeks ago."

"What's the address?" Robert asked as he grabbed a pen from the counter.

"How did he sell a book, if the bookstore wasn't even here in the first place—at least not until we came?" whispered Katie to Sam. "Seems I asked a similar question before. Just one more thing I don't understand."

"I've quit questioning stuff," said Sam. "Nothing makes any sense anyway, so why question when I only get a weird answer that leads to another crazy question. We have a talking cat, a Gargoyle that also talks and a witch here. So I've given up trying to understand!"

Merlin said the only address he had was Dowershire Lane across town. Robert wrote it down on a piece of paper and put it into his pocket.

"Okay, let's go."

"Go where, and what are we going to do once we get there?" asked Sam sensibly.

"We have to get that book back, somehow. We'll figure that out on the way."

"I have contacts over in that area," said Sherlock. "I'll get in touch and perhaps they can help you. They don't speak English, but I will tell them what you need and they'll know what to do."

"Thank you, Sherlock. You have all been good friends to Willie," said Robert.

"We won't be seeing you again, so good luck and tell Willie, we miss our good times together," said Sherlock as he and the hundred or so cats, with stripes and spots, short tails and long tails, filed past Robert, Sam, Katie and Merlin and out the door, disappearing into thin air.

Robert, Sam, Katie, Hilga and Gargoyle caught a

double-decker bus, and with a transfer to another bus, continued on to Dowershire Hills, then on to Dowershire Lane. Katie noticed the other passengers looking at Hilga, carrying what appeared to be a weird piece of cement, so she put her sweater that she carried, over Gargoyle.

They entered a very quaint neighborhood, mostly attached houses with flower gardens in the small front yards. As they rode along, they noticed an occasional cat running alongside the bus, then more cats and this time a few dogs joining the bunch. They came to Dowershire Lane and got off at the bus stop.

"I wonder which way now?" Robert said as he watched the cats, fifteen or twenty of them. They would suddenly run a few feet, stop, turn around and look at him. Then they would run further, stop, turn around and look again.

"They want us to follow," decided Robert.

They all went a little further along the block, when the cats stopped and sat down in front of a particular two-story house in a row of buildings that all looked the same.

"How do they know which house belongs to the Bellows?" Katie looked on in awe.

"They just *know*. This is a different world we're in right now, Katie," answered Robert.

"Okay, now what?" asked Sam. "Those cats are just sitting there. Do they have a plan on how to get into the house? I can't believe I just said that."

"I feel uncomfortable just standing out here, like we're loitering or something," said Katie.

"We are . . . wait, the gray cat with the white spots is running toward the gate," remarked Robert.

The other cats quickly ran out of sight into the

bushes along the side of the fence. The front door of the chosen house opened and a little boy appeared holding a toy truck, which he placed on the ground. He sat down beside it and began to play. Slowly, the gray cat walked up beside him and began to purr, while rubbing its head along the boy's arm. He petted the cat and it nuzzled its face into his chest. He smiled, picked up the cat, and went to the door, opened it and went inside. Well, the problem of how to get into the house was solved, by a cunning cat.

"I guess we'll just have to wait and see what happens next."

About five minutes went by, when Robert noticed some of the dogs and cats running down the block and around the corner.

"Where's Hilga?" asked Robert. "Gargoyle is here, but she's not. She was here a minute ago, so what's she up to now?"

Meantime, inside the house, the housekeeper told the boy that he could give the gray cat a bowl of warm milk, but then it would have to go back outside. After all, the housekeeper said, it is an alley cat and she didn't want to have to clean up after it.

"Kitty," as the boy called him, licked up the milk while in a state of ecstacy. *I've never known such a heavenly taste,* the cat thought to himself. Then feeling all warm and fuzzy, he curled up by the kitchen stove and began to fall asleep. Suddenly he woke with a start, remembering why he had come into the house to begin with. He then carefully sneaked past the housekeeper, preparing tea for the lady of the house, who at the time was relaxing in a bubble bath upstairs.

Kitty began searching around each room, darting from curtain to curtain and under tables and chairs to keep from being seen, since he wasn't supposed to be left in the house.

In the library, the nanny had fallen asleep in a big easy chair, so he crept silently past her, jumping up on tables to gain a good vantage point. Examining the books on the shelves, none had the name of *Water Life.* Jumping from one shelf to another, Kitty lost his balance and accidentally knocked over a small vase, causing it to crash to the wood floor. The nanny jumped up from the chair and began yelling and chasing him.

He dashed out the library door and up the stairs to the second floor, with the nanny and the housekeeper running after, waving a broom. He quickly ran through an open door, into a bedroom, with a canopy bed and heavy drapes at the windows.

With the pursuers close behind, Kitty made a dash for another partially open door. Inside, he landed on a small rug and slid across the floor hitting the side of a large tub, flipping himself up over the side and down "KERPLOP!" through a large mound of soap bubbles, into the water below.

Also in the tub was the lady of the house, wearing an eye mask and relaxing in the warm water, with her head leaning on a small inflated plastic pillow against the back of the tub. Hearing the *kerplop,* she sat up, listening. She decided it was nothing and leaned back.

Then, she sat up again and screamed that something touched her on her leg! Kitty, all covered with soap suds, stood up in the water on his hind legs, leaning his front paws against the side of the tub. He gasped a big gulp of air and turned to look at where the scream came from. He looked square into big black eyes with lace around them.

"RRROOWWRR!"

He then jumped straight up out of the tub, just as the

nanny and the housekeeper came running into the bathroom. Kitty scrambled, sliding through their legs and out the door, hearing that awful scream. He looked back and saw both the nanny and the housekeeper collide in a heap on the floor next to the tub and that screaming lady with the big black eyes had grabbed the shower curtain and pulled it down covering all three of them.

Kitty found another open door leading into another bedroom. There were small airplanes hanging from the ceiling, along with toy trucks and stuffed animals on the floor. Kitty jumped up onto the desk situated in front of a window that opened from the middle, but was latched shut. Outside he could see Hilga hanging for dear life on a slim tree branch, that almost reached the window, along with awkward fluttering of her wings to stay aloft. She was motioning for Kitty to look under his own paws. He was standing on top of the book, and the gold key (which had become the bookmark), was sticking out of the end of the book.

When he saw the book, he became so excited, that he began jumping up and down on his little kitty feet. Hilga, waving both her arms in a fury, motioned for him to open the window.

Kitty reached up and flipped up the latch, causing the window to open outward. He then picked up the book—with the key still inside—and handed it to Hilga, who with relief, lowered herself down to the ground with those wavering wings.

While all of this was going on, a chorus of barking was heard. Sam ran down the block and around the corner to the alley behind the row of houses. Soon he returned and said, "You won't believe this, but those dogs have all the cats cornered and they are barking at them and the cats are howling and hissing creating a real commotion! I think they're doing that on purpose, just so the residents will go out to see what's going on. They are distracting them, so we can do whatever it is we're going to do out here in the front, which by the way, is WHAT? We've been waiting out here for over thirty minutes. What is going on inside?"

"I don't know any more than you, Sam. I just know that these cats and dogs know what they're doing and we have to trust them," said Robert, thinking that it was a pretty feeble answer.

Because of all the barking and commotion in the back of the houses, the housekeeper, nanny and the cook all went out the back door to investigate. This enabled Kitty to make his way downstairs without being seen. He hid behind the back door, waiting for the nanny and the housekeeper and the cook to come back inside, allowing Kitty to make his great escape outside. Which is just what happened.

Kitty ran down the steps into the back yard and gave the "okay" sign to the yowling and hissing dogs and cats. They all suddenly stopped making their disturbances and sat down together, totally confusing the people who had gathered around them.

In the meantime, Robert, Katie, Sam and Gargoyle stood in the street feeling a little conspicuous, when a movement turned their attention to the window on the second floor. The gray cat with the spots was seen handing a book to Hilga, who was perched in the tree next to the window. Then they watched her awkwardly lower herself down with fluttering wings. She proudly scurried to Robert and gave him the book.

"Things have quieted down in back," Hilga said. "We'd better get out of here."

Robert walked up to the front step of Bellows's house

and left the book minus the key. As they started to walk away toward the corner to catch the bus, they saw the gray cat with the white spots run from the back, and join with the other cats and dogs.

"Let's go!" said Robert. They all walked quickly to the corner to catch the next bus.

"Hey!"

"Hilga, you left Gargoyle again."

As they climbed onto the bus, they looked out the windows and saw the dogs and cats all sitting together swishing their tails as if to say goodbye.

"I will never look at dogs and cats the same way again," said Sam.

20
The Transport

When they reached the hotel, Robert lifted the small leather bag from his pocket and spread the dust on the table. They watched as words began to form. "CEN-TR S-TON-OF-F-RY RI . . ."

"We're losing the dust, it's trying to tell us what to do. I think it's saying the 'CENTER STONE OF THE FAIRY RING.' We're going to have to hurry. I think this is the time to act!"

Katie and Sam looked at each other and then at Robert.

"What, Robert, what are you saying?" asked Katie.

"I'm saying that it's time to get to the ring before it's too late! This time, I intend to go to 'Grindle.' Are you two coming?" He grabbed the bag of dust and the key and left the room. Hilga, carrying Gargoyle, rushed out after him.

"I'm going too," said Sam. "I've seen too much to quit now." He also walked out of the room, leaving Katie staring after them.

"We have to get to the rental car agency before they close. It's almost four o'clock now," said Robert as he waved for a cab. He was disappointed that Katie had not followed. But just as they were stepping into the cab, Katie hollered, "If you guys think you're going to some 'fairy land' without me, you're all nuts!"

"Where is this place, we're heading for?" asked Sam, as he settled in the back seat of the rental car. Hilga and Gargoyle sat next to him and he glanced at them now and then wondering why she didn't just fly.

"We're going southwest toward the town of Trowbridge," answered Robert. A map had been left on the seat when Sam got into the car. He picked it up and scanned it until he came to the small town of Trowbridge.

"There it is. And, not far from Stonehenge. I've always wanted to see Stonehenge," he mumbled.

"I think you will tonight, Sam," said Robert through a smile.

Sam could hear a faint cackle coming from Hilga, making him turn to look at her, and thinking she was so annoying. Katie sat beside Robert in the front seat, in a trance-like stupor, wondering what was reality anyway?

Everyone was quiet for the rest of the trip, which took three hours. The weather was misty with threatening clouds. As they came to the fork in the road, one to Trowbridge and the other to Wiltshire, Robert turned the car in the direction of Trowbridge.

"Hey, this is the way to Stonehenge," remarked Sam as he sat up to observe the horizon more clearly. "Too bad it's so dark, but maybe I'll get to see it after all!"

Robert turned onto the road leading to the large stones that were now looming ominously against the dark sky.

"Hey great, ole buddy, but do we have time to stop here? We don't have much time to get to the . . . ring." Sam found difficulty in referring to it as a "fairy" ring.

"Yep."

"Cackle, Cackle."

Sam frowned at Hilga.

Robert stopped the car in the parking lot and got out, with Sam following. Hilga picked up Gargoyle and also got out.

"I'll wait here," said Katie, wondering why Hilga had to go along too, hauling that heavy lump of cement.

"No, don't wait in the car, Katie, come with us," urged Robert. She reluctantly followed, thinking they were wasting time. But she was glad she did; Stonehenge was quite magnificent.

As they entered the center of the ring of stones, the travelers felt very small and insignificant. Robert looked around for the center stone, that the dust had spoken of. Sam was running from one end to the other marveling at the sight and Katie stood in one spot turning around to take it all in.

"It's not here," said Hilga. "And it's almost midnight!"

"What's not here?" asked Sam as he got closer to them.

"The center stone."

"The center what?"

"The center stone."

"What?" Katie came closer and her eyes got bigger as she gradually understood what Robert was saying.

Sam looked at Robert, then at the huge ring of stones. He looked back at Robert and shook his head.

"I don't believe it. It's not . . . It *can't* be. It's Stonehenge. STONEHENGE!" He turned around squinting at the huge stones, just shaking his head.

"I thought the 'fairy ring ' would be a small ring of rocks, the kind you used to see in children's books . . . But *this!* This thing means business! Nooooo!"

Just as he spoke, the stones lit up like spotlights and a bolt of lightning struck just in front of them, causing them all to be thrown onto the ground. When they looked back, the "Center Stone" had plopped down where they had been standing. It was a large, flat, glowing stone with an indentation in the top in the shape of the key. The lightning in the sky was becoming more intense and the thunder rumbled!

"Grab hands, everybody," hollered Robert over the booming noise. "This is it! When I place the key into the stone, we're going to be transported to Grindle!"

Everyone grabbed each other's hands; Robert, Sam, Katie and Hilga, who with her spare hand, held Gargoyle tight against her. Robert carefully placed the key into the stone. The raging thundering and the winds suddenly stopped. The inside of the ring lit up like fire and a small whirling sound began. The wind picked up and formed a funnel around them. Katie panicked and let go of Sam and Hilga's hands.

"I can't do this!" she yelled.

"We're not going without you!" said Sam, as he quickly grabbed her hand just as the funnel picked them up and they all disappeared into the night.

All—except Hilga, who could not grab Katie's hand in time.

Everything went quiet and darkness came. All alone on the ground where she was thrown after losing her grip on anyone's hand, sat Hilga, a sad, disappointed and a noticeably haggard old witch.

"Aaaaaaahhhhhhh!" she screeched. "Not again! I will never get to go home! And neither will you, you ugly old piece of concrete!" She looked around, but did not see the gargoyle.

"THE GARGOYLE WENT—AND I *DIDN'T?* BUT I WAS *HOLDING* HIM! Aaaaaaaaaahhhhhhhhhh!"

Hilga sat on the grass for at least an hour, feeling dejected and blurting an occasional "Aaaahhhh." She finally composed herself, got up, brushed herself off and said, "Well, I still have the china shop. Or rather, what's his name's shop. What will I do with him this time?"

21
Grindle

It was one year ago when Willie the cat was successfully transported as Prince William, back to Grindle to reclaim the throne. But upon his arrival, the former Wizard Grizzard's apprentice, Gerard, who was taking over as Wizard, was flying through the forest hunting a rare butterfly. By chance, he happened onto the scene of the fairy ring and the transportation of William. When William was fully materialized, it took him a minute to be able to move his body. He could see Gerard coming toward him, but by the time he could move, he was enveloped in a butterfly net.

"Do you have to carry such a large net, Gerard? The butterflies are quite small, you know."

"Oh, but look what I have captured in my large net," he replied. "What a surprise for King Grizzard! And pray tell, what are you doing here? I thought the King had finally disposed of you altogether. And for your information, I carry large nets in case I happen upon a *Beautifus Taradactus.* They are large, you know. And it would complete my collection."

"You are weird, Gerard! And your 'King Grizzard' is not really the King. He was not chosen by my father. *I* was! And he was not properly crowned according to the book of the Kingdom, so it doesn't count."

"Well, we'll see," said Gerard as he lifted the net from William and took flight to Grindle.

"Do you still know how to fly, William?"

William fluffed his wings and fluttered them into a lift-off. When he reached the castle, he flew right onto the terrace of the royal chamber and into the open windows. Grizzard jumped a foot when he saw William. He became so enraged upon seeing him that he raised his staff and pulled lightning bolts from everywhere, setting them off all over the kingdom. People were scattering and ducking under tables and even chairs.

"How did you get back here? I, as King, don't even know how *I* would return, once I had gone from Grindle! Guards!" Grizzard yelled. All of the guards were hesitant to respond because the real King had returned and they didn't want any problems with him in case he managed to get the throne back.

"Guards! Take him to the Tower at once!"

Again, no one moved, except one meek guard who always huddled in the background. He was afraid of Grizzard, so thought he would favor reacting, rather than being turned into a hideous toad or something equally distasteful. He raised his spear and moved toward William.

"Wait!" demanded Grizzard. "We would only have to feed him if he's a man . . . but a cat only needs water and an occasional fairy mouse . . . and we're always catching *them* in the kitchen . . ." Grizzard brought one of the lightning bolts from above and turned William back into Willie.

The meek guard put down his spear and gathered Willie into his arms and carried him to the Tower.

"Take care of yourself, William. I will see that you have enough to eat."

The tower was the highest of the castle, with no way of escape. The only window was low and had a ledge big enough for Willie to while away his days sitting, looking out over his Kingdom. He hoped that one day Robert would come to Grindle and rescue him.

As time went by, all of the people knew Willie/William was a prisoner, but had no power or way to release him. The key to the Tower was transported to Hilga for safekeeping, but at the time, she did not know that it was also a way to return to Grindle. And of course, she didn't have any fairy dust to help her out . . .

Now, one year later, in the same spot where William was brought back, four objects began to appear. One by one, human forms began taking shape—Gargoyle last. They stood motionless, in awe of the sights that surrounded them. They stood in the middle of the magnificent Stonehenge that was standing in the formation that, they supposed, was the way it first was. Plants of some species filled the inside of the ring, with large flower buds that seemed to sway in the morning mist. Outside of the ring was the forest. Katie thought it was the most beautiful sight she'd ever seen, lush with plants, ferns, giant toadstools and pools of clear blue water with waterfalls flowing from cliffs above. Orchids and other exotic botanicals carried the scent of perfume-filled air. It had been silent when they first arrived, but the sounds of birds began to be heard. Flickering lights, like fireflies, dotted the scene. It was early morning and the forest was coming alive with activity.

"You have your mouth open again, Katie," said Sam.

"I can't believe it. It's spectacular! Everything seems so big; the ferns, flowers, even the toadstools are huge . . . almost like . . . we're . . . *small.*" Katie took Robert's arm and looked at him, waiting for a response.

"I don't know, Katie. Maybe we are small, we're in a fairyland and I guess fairies were always supposed to be small. This is truly an enchanted place. What do we do now, Hilga? You'll have to be our guide."

Robert turned around.

"Hilga? HILGA! Oh, no, she didn't make it? How did Gargoyle get through and not Hilga? She was holding him, for heaven's sake! I *promised* her!"

"Hilga! You crazy old hag!" yelled Gargoyle "You just have to be here. We're a team now, you shriveled-up old crone!" Gargoyle lowered his head and looked very sad.

"I can't believe she didn't make it," said Katie. "It's my fault. I let go of her hand! I didn't mean for her not to come with us. Besides . . . Yeah, but how DID Gargoyle get though and not her?"

"Maybe she's around here somewhere. She could have dropped somewhere else," said Sam as he began looking around, behind trees and under giant ferns. "And maybe not!

"But maybe there's a way to bring her here, yet," said Sam. "Somebody *must* know what to do; maybe Willie? We have to find Willie."

Sam picked up Gargoyle and they began to make their way into the forest. As they walked a short distance, constantly looking around and admiring the sights, they made their way toward what appeared to be an edge of the forest. A meadow flooded with grasses and flowers spread out before them. Dewdrops shimmered on the huge flower petals, and the bees, equally as big, began buzzing from flower to flower on their morning rounds.

The sky was blue with fluffy clouds here and there, and birds of great size were swooping down, as if to get a better look at these people with no wings.

As the travelers made their way along the edge of the forest, they could see in the distance a castle looming above what appeared to be other dwellings. The castle was set against high cliffs of craggy stone with plant life above and below. This appeared to be a fairy tale picture, and they were *in it.*

The little flickering lights that Katie had seen earlier came closer and closer. She noticed that they looked like large butterflies, but different than any butterflies she'd seen before. She reached out and cupped her hands, catching one. When she opened them, her eyes widened and she tried to speak, but could only gasp.

"Robert! Sam!" she finally squealed. "Look!" Sitting in her hand was a tiny fairy with transparent wings of silver and gold.

Robert and Sam stared. They were speechless.

Finally . . . "Are they all this small?" queried Sam. "Look, more of them—they're flying all around us!"

They were in different sizes, but mostly small. The tiny fairy in Katie's hand stood up, fluttered her wings and off she went. In an instant, as if by pre-arrangement, they were all gone from the area.

"Where did they go?"

"I don't know, but they just vanished." Robert took Katie's hand and they continued on toward the castle.

As they entered the gates of Grindle, people were beginning to gather to observe the three of them. They recognized Gargoyle and seemed happy to see him. Walking slowly through the crowd, Robert, Katie and Sam looked in amazement at the people who were really fairies, with beautiful shimmering wings.

"They have *wings! All* of them! Wait till I tell the guys back home!" remarked Sam.

"I don't think you'll want to do that, Sam," advised Robert.

Meanwhile, in the castle, Grizzard was going into his Wizard room to clean out his Wizard stuff. He didn't want to leave too many of his secrets for Gerard, when he took over as Wizard. He planned to announce Gerard as the new Wizard in a couple of days, and wanted things in order. As he worked, he noticed the "Invader Indicator" button flashing on and off. He quickly pushed the button and the screen before him lit up, focusing on three and a quarter objects coming into view.

"What is that?" he exclaimed. "I'll have to get the 'Conjures' to look into this matter." He crossed over to another machine bearing the trade name "Conjure-Upper," to conjure up the "Conjures." The "Conjures" turned out to be a dozen misfits, who were released from the Moon flowers on the night when an eclipse of the moon occurred. Because of the eclipse, a group of dark and grouchy fairies appeared instead of the regular Grindle fairies. They lived in another part of the valley, because they couldn't stand how prissy and happy the other fairies were. And, they didn't like Grizzard very much and were cranky because he was the cause of their friend Hilga being zapped away. Grizzard called them the "Conjures," first because he didn't know what else to call them, and secondly, the fact that he had to "conjure" them up from the Conjure-Upper machine.

"Hey, Jasper, old Grizzard is conjuring us up again! Wonder what he wants this time," said Trappie the Conjure to a friend.

"Probably something as stupid as it was the last time. Like swatting the fairy flies away from his fairy horses. I don't know why he has to ride horses anyway, he can fly wherever he wants to go!" laughed Jasper. One by one the fairies got up and took off toward the castle.

Grizzard was drinking a cup of tea, waiting for the Conjures, when suddenly one swooped through the window, startling him causing him to spill his beverage.

"I've got to keep that blasted window closed!" snarled Grizzard to himself. One by one they came flying through the terrace window, hovering above him with wide-spread wings. *A little mean-looking,* thought Grizzard.

"What is it?" asked Crow, the head Conjure.

"There are some invaders here in Grindle. I want you to find them and bring them to me!"

"What have they done?" asked Jasper.

"Nothing, yet."

"Then why . . . ?"

"Just find them and bring them to me!" Grizzard demanded.

"Jeeesh!"

Off the Conjures flew out of the wizard's windows. They went from one part of Grindle to the other. Then in the center square, they saw them. Two males, one female—and what was that other thing?

The crowd of fairies that had gathered around the travelers was inquisitive, touching them as if they weren't real. The fairies looked for wings, but the travelers didn't have any. Slowly, they began to talk to the travelers, of course speaking in English, since they all spoke many languages. The travelers were asked their names, and where they were from. Katie noted that the fairies were the same size as she and Robert and Sam—but they told her "no, that she was THEIR size."

She noticed that some had beautiful long golden hair, and some had red hair, or brown or black hair. *Just like us,* she thought. Except for wings! And they had such smooth skin. The males were equally handsome. They wore tunic tops with tights and the females wore flowing garments that seemed to be made of silk. Their wings were exquisite looking as though they were spun from silver and gold. They also spoke quite eloquently.

Sam looked up and saw the dark figures flying down toward them.

"Robert, Katie, quick, run!" But before they could comprehend what he was trying to tell them, the Conjures were upon them.

"Hey, that's ole Gargoyle!" yelled Conjure Stanley. "I wondered what happened to him!" They swooped down to the square and landed in a circle around Robert, Sam and Katie.

"Robert!" Katie ducked behind him at the sight of the foreboding creatures with the black wings.

"You have to come with us," demanded Crow.

"Hey, Gargoyle, you devil, you! Where have you been? The castle corner top hasn't been the same without you up there with that snarly face," remarked Stanley.

"What is that? A duck foot?"

"Oh, Hilga and I have been hanging out with British royalty! You idiot! Where do you *think* I have been! Thanks to Grizzard!"

"Well, at least you haven't lost your charming personality!" returned Stanley.

"Where to?" interrupted Robert.

"Grizzard wants to see you."

"We came to see William. Where is he?"

"You'll see him soon enough," said Crow. He grabbed Katie and Gargoyle and lifted off the ground. Katie screamed for Robert as he was also thrown over Jasper's back. Stanley grabbed Sam and off they all went to Grizzard's terrace.

"So, you are Robert. I've heard about you." Grizzard paced back and forth and around the huddled three. "To what do I owe this visit?"

"We came to find William and set him free to be the rightful King of Grindle!" Robert boldly stated.

"Oh?"

"Where is he?"

"You'll see. Off to the Tower with them, Conjures, until I've decided what to do with them!"

The Conjures shrugged and politely escorted Robert, Sam and Katie up stairs, down corridors, around corners and up stairs again.

"You know, we really don't care all that much for Grizzard. He was always such a bully and never treated our friend Hilga right," explained Crow.

"She really isn't as tough as she sounds. She just tries to live up a witch's reputation."

"Crow, can we transport Hilga? She was going to come back with us, but somehow Gargoyle made it and she didn't. We promised her."

"No, you can't—it takes that golden key. The one that locked up William and the one that Grizzard zapped to Hilga to keep. We always knew that key was it, the one that did everything, but we never told anyone because we'd have people and things being zapped here and there all the time and what chaos that would be! Anyway, we need that key in order to make a transport. Do you know what happened to it after you arrived?"

“No, we don’t. It didn’t come with us. It must be in limbo out there, maybe because the transport wasn’t complete when Hilga was left behind.”

“Which means the transport mode is still activated,” Crow said in deep concentration.

“And if the center stone appears with the key, anything or anyone can be unknowingly caught in the transport. If Hilga has gone from the area, we have to find her and get her back to the fairy ring!”

As they reached the tower, Willie had just caught a fairy mouse and had it in his mouth, ready to partake of the delicious morsel. He heard steps coming toward him, so he sat up straight, fairy mouse wings sticking out from both sides of his own mouth.

“Is Willie in here, too?” Robert asked.

“*Robbbleerbt . . . pffft.* ROBERT! Is that you?” yelled Willie, as he spit out the mouse. “I knew you would come!” He was jumping up and down behind the cell bars.

“Willie! You’re the same ole cat I remember! I didn’t know you had been here all year, or I would’ve come sooner.”

“You wouldn’t have been able to. You can only make the trip once a year, Robert. But things haven’t been too bad. I just whiled away my time, learning mouse talk. Too bad I had to eat one occasionally. And . . . I was waiting for you. I knew you wouldn’t be able to stand not knowing if there really was a Grindle or not, and apparently you couldn’t, cause here you are! And whom did you bring with you? I bet this one is Katie and that one, Sam. Robert told me a lot about you two. What happened to Hilga and Gargoyle? They were a pair, huh?”

“Same Willie, talks a blue streak,” smiled Robert.

“Shut your mouth, Katie,” reminded Sam.

“You people will be in this cell across from William.

We're going to have to shut the door, which will lock automatically. If we don't, Grizzard will check it, to make sure it's locked, anyway. In the meantime, we will check out a way to get Hilga back."

Crow and the other Conjures departed, leaving the four of them locked in the two rooms of the Tower.

"Gargoyle came with us, Willie. I think Grizzard will probably put him back on the castle top. I guess all we can do now is wait for the Conjures to help us."

Robert told Willie everything that had taken place on his return to London and to the present regarding Hilga, Gargoyle, Sherlock and all of Willie's cat friends. Katie and Sam settled back on a pile of clean straw that felt like a feather bed and watched and listened to Robert and his friend, the talking cat named Willie.

22
Zap, Again

"The coast is clear, Crow," whispered Conjure Jiggers. "Grizzard is in his chambers, listening to Chopin. We'll have to hurry, before he realizes he hasn't sent us back to the valley."

The Conjures tiptoed to the Wizard room and quietly unlatched the door. Jasper wondered why Grizzard hadn't kept the room of secret goodies locked, as he did everything else.

"Check that corner and I'll check this one," ordered Crow.

"He sure has a lot of junk!"

"Just look for something that we can use."

"Eeeek! A fairy spider!"

"Look! Here's an 'Other Time and Place' viewing machine," said Conjure Trappy. He pushed the button underneath the screen and it lit up. Lines appeared and then blurred pictures slowly came into focus.

"Hey, there's Big Ben!" observed Stanley.

Crow tried more buttons, finally pinpointing a street full of shops.

"I wonder why it's bringing up this particular street. There's what looks like a china shop. It is! AND THERE'S HILGA! What the heck is Hilga doing in a china shop?"

"Well, she couldn't just hang out on the street corners

leaning up against street lamps, you know," replied Jasper.

"Eeeyuk! What a picture THAT paints in my mind!" mumbled Stanley.

"I just hope that center stone appears again."

"Okay, now we have to figure how to get her to the fairy ring. I wonder what this button does . . ."

Hilga had resigned herself to waiting, perhaps another year to, with luck, find a way to go home. So she made her way back to the china shop to a still bewildered looking shopkeeper. He looked at her, as she entered the shop, with some glimmer of recognition, when suddenly with the waving of her arms and a "HOCUS POCUS, CHANGE HIM ONCE MORE, INTO A FIGURE OF CHINA FOLK LORE." And "POOF" he again entered the world of stationary items, sitting on the same glass shelf as before.

Hilga took up shopkeeping, absentmindedly wearing her big floppy hat. She opened the shop for business, just as a flurry of tourists, from a tour bus, came toward the door. They chattered as they looked at all the fine china. Among them was a young boy, about twelve years old, who seemed quite taken with the figurines, representing people of different lands and cultures. One in particular, was an Oriental man, who seemed to have a puzzling expression. The boy pressed his nose on the glass and peered into the figurine's eyes. It blinked at him.

"Yikes!" He jumped and ran to his mother and pulled on her arm.

"What is it?" the mother asked.

"Over there, those figures. See the one standing by the Indian one? Look at it. It blinked at me! See?"

"Don't tell stories; I've told you about telling stories, Martin," she annoyedly said.

"But it *did!* You have to go see it. It *did!*"

"I don't see anything, stop pulling on my arm!"

Martin slowly walked back to the glass case, stopped and looked back trying to get his mother's attention, but she was busy talking to the other ladies. Suddenly, Hilga, seeing him staring at the shopkeeper, appeared before him.

"Can I help you, little boy?" she asked, wringing her hands.

He jumped, backed up a couple steps. He thought she looked spooky, but he was about to point to the figurine, when "POOF," Hilga vanished right before his eyes.

"AAAAAhhhhhhhhh!" the boy screamed. He took more steps backward, coming into contact with the glass shelves. He turned and looked squarely into the eyes of the figurine. Suddenly the glass case shattered, crashing to the floor—and there stood the man figurine, looming large before him.

"AAAAAhhhhhhhhh!"

23
The Reunion

Hilga was deposited in the grass with a thud! "OOMPH!"

"Jeez! Careful! I'm an old woman, for heaven's sake." She looked around her and saw that she was sitting in the middle of the Fairy Ring.

"What am I doing here? How did I get here?" A big smile lit up her face. "Am I going home to Grindle after all?"

"Okay," said Crow. "We have her at the fairy ring. Now, we have to get her here, but I don't know what to do next. Here's another button and it's a red one. Maybe that's the biggie." Crow slowly pushed the red button and waited. He could see Hilga standing there, as if waiting for whatever to happen next.

"KERPLOP!" The center stone appeared, causing Hilga to flip over and sprawl face-down on the grass. Still lying in the middle of the stone was the gold key!

"Okay, now, Hilga—the rest is your move."

Crow and the other Conjures watched intently as Hilga stared at the gold key for a moment, then picked it up out of the resting place. She then carefully laid it back down into the indentation, the Conjures held their breath . . . then the silence came. Then, as before, the winds picked up and began to swirl into a funnel, picking Hilga off the ground, twirling and enveloping around her until she disappeared from the center of the ring. Then all was quiet. The old witch and the golden key had been successfully transported back to Grindle.

"We did it! We did it! Quick, let's get out of here before Grizzard hears us!"

One by one the Conjures flew out of the terrace window and into the sky.

Grizzard abruptly sat up from a slight slumber. Standing before him was the old witch who had vanished so long ago.

"Hilga? Is that you?"

"Grizzard, you do have to be more careful with those lightning bolts, you know. You could hurt someone the way you zap those things around! Look what happened to Gargoyle and me. By the way, where is Gargoyle?"

"He's back on the castle top. I had the royal mortar men repair its ears and cement it back onto the tower top. How did it get nicks in its ears, anyway? How did you get back here, and where have you been?"

"Gargoyle and I ended up on the streets of London, actually in the Queen's garden, thanks to you. But we're back now, and I understand those three musketeers got here ahead of me. Ummm . . . what happened to them?"

"They're in the Tower."

"Good! Good place for them. It took a while, but I finally convinced them—including all those cats, that I wasn't so bad—and I tricked them into trusting me, and bringing me along. Uhh . . . which Tower, we have three of them?"

"The North Tower."

"Oh. Well I've had a long day. I'll be in my chambers."

"Hilga?"

"Yes?" She turned around, peering at Grizzard from underneath her floppy hat.

"Where is the key?"

"What key?"

"You know what key!"

"Oh, *that* key," she said with a chuckle. "Silly me, I must've left it at the landing. I don't seem to have it." She searched her dress pockets and patted herself, looking very innocent. "I'll come back tomorrow and try to find it," she said in a consoling manner.

"I want that key tomorrow morning!" demanded Grizzard.

Hilga smiled as she bid him goodnight and slipped out the door. She went to her chambers and locked the door. She then lifted from her shoe the golden key and laid it on the table. She was pleased with herself, because she had fooled Grizzard. But then, for a Wizard, he wasn't very smart in the first place.

Later, that evening, when everyone had gone to bed, Hilga quietly got up and slipped the golden key into her pocket. She then left her room and without a sound made her way down the corridors, up the stairs, around the corners, up more stairs and into the North Tower.

Willie sat straight up from a sound sleep. He heard someone's footsteps outside the big heavy door that led into the cells.

"Hey, Robert, wake up! Someone's coming."

Robert, Sam and Katie all sat up, listening, wondering who would be coming to the Tower this time of night. A figure dressed in a black hood entered. Suddenly the figure threw off the hooded cloak and whispered, "Ta da!"

"Hilga!"

"SSShhh!"

"Hilga, how did you find us? And how did you get here? We are so sorry about the transport. The Conjures promised to help and they obviously did because here you are!"

"Well, I'm not really sure how I got here, but the Conjures are good friends to me and I'm sure they did help. And I went directly to Grizzard and gave him a big story about how glad I was to see him and he said that he had you all locked up. You'd've been proud of me. Anyway, he trusts me, the idiot, and now, since I have the key, I'm giving it to you and when the time is right, you can all escape."

"But what about Grizzard and his cohort, Gerard?"

"The Conjures and I will dispose of them. In the meantime, I have to go make plans."

She turned to go, when Willie said, "Hilga, you are a good friend, thank you. And when I am King, you will have your place as the 'Kingdom Wizard.' "

Hilga's eyes lit up and she smiled. "Toodle-oo!"

Out the Tower door she went quietly, so as not to wake the Tower guard.

"What did you do to that witch?" Willie asked. "She's nice!"

"I think she was probably nice to begin with, but had an image to live up to," Robert said as they settled back onto the straw.

"You know, this straw is like a feather bed. I wonder why it's so soft here."

"It's fairy straw, Katie," replied Sam.

"Goodnight, Willie. We'll plan our strategy in the morning." Robert put the key into his pocket. Willie jumped upon the window ledge and looked out at the moonlit village below the castle. He was a contented cat. He had his friends beside him and all would be well.

24
Ha-Wah-Hee

The next morning, Hilga went directly to Grizzard's chamber and tapped lightly on the door. No answer. She tapped again, this time harder. And still no answer. She quietly lifted the handle on the door and peeked inside.

What a mess! she thought to herself, as she glanced around the room. *He has junk everywhere, just like a kid.* She then saw the Wizard still asleep in his giant bed. *He even wears his crown to bed? Not only that, but he snores!* Carefully pulling the door shut, she wedged her broom handle into the latch, securing it tight.

Inside the Wizard room, she went to the Conjure-Upper machine and pushed the button. The screen showed the typical snow and then it cleared, showing her friends, all still asleep in the trees. She pushed another button sounding an alarm and they all jumped—a couple falling off the branches, KERPLOP onto the ground.

"Dad gummit! What does he want now!" hollered Jasper, as he clung to a branch above his head.

"Come on, let's go and get this over with."

"He doesn't even give us time to wake up and eat and brush our teeth! Not only that, but I . . ."

"Oh, shut up and let's go!"

One by one the Conjures flew into the terrace window of the Wizard room.

"Hilga! Good to see you!"

"Hi, boys, I'm back."

"Where's old Grizzard?"

"Still asleep."

"We missed you and all our capers that we did together. Tell us what you did while you and Gargoyle were away. By the way, where is Gargoyle?"

"He had some repair work done and is back on the castle top. I became a teeny, weeny bit fond of him while we were in London. Anyway, here's what I want you guys to do."

The fairy birds were chirping especially loud this morning, thought a sleepy Grizzard, as he buried his head in the bedcovers. Seeing that he was not getting up, the birds flew into the chamber and perched on top of the canopy bed where they chirped even louder.

"Good grief!" Grizzard sat up. "Nobody can sleep with this racket going on!" He stomped out of bed, threw on his robe and fluffed his wings. He paced back and forth, trying to decide what to do with his captives in the Tower. The only one he could trust was Gerard, and even then he wasn't sure about him. He would have to go to the transport center and find that elusive key that Hilga had so carelessly left behind.

He rang the bell for his morning tea to be brought in. When it didn't come, he got angry and yanked on the door latch. Nothing. He pulled again, but it was shut tight.

"Now, what's wrong with this dag-blasted door?" he yelled. "The whole castle is in need of repair!"

Once more, he yanked on the door latch and it opened, throwing him across the room in a heap. He looked up and saw Hilga, with her broom in her hand. Beside her were Crow, Willie, Robert, Sam, Katie and the rest of the Conjures.

"What's the meaning of this? How did they get out of their cells? Gerard?" Willie sauntered up to Grizzard and sat down.

"Now then, Grizzard, you are to turn me back into William. If you don't, our friend Hilga will turn you into a Warblink! And you know what the Conjures' favorite food is?"

"Warblinks?"

"Yeah."

"What the heck is a Warblink?" asked Sam.

"Conjures' favorite food," answered Hilga.

"Yeah," interrupted Jasper. "They taste like chicken."

"Are you crazy? I am finally king, and I don't plan to give it up just because you think she can turn me into a, what was that called . . .?"

Hilga stepped forward and began to wave her arms, mumbling some gibberish.

"Stop! Okay, okay," yelled Grizzard. "But first I want to know what will happen to me? Can I be the Kingdom Wizard again?"

"No, I want that!" snarled Hilga, stomping her feet.

"You're crazy! . . . you aren't even very good with incantations and you were always clumsy at snagging lightning bolts. You failed that course, remember?" snickered Grizzard.

"HOCUS, POCUS, RINKY DINK. TURN HIM INTO A WARBL . . ."

"Wait!"

"Oh, now what?"

"Okay, you can be Wizard, but what will become of

me?" Grizzard lowered his head, looking sad, peering out of the corner of his eyes to see if he was gaining sympathy.

"I don't trust you, Grizzard. I will have to think about that."

"Well?" demanded an impatient Willie.

Grizzard sighed and decided, oh well, being King was enough of a big responsibility and he was really too lazy to be "kinging" all over the place. He reached up with his staff, and a bolt of lightning appeared. He brought it down and, with it, touched Willie. Robert, Katie and Sam jumped as the thunder boomed and the flash encircled Willie. Then it was suddenly still and there in Willie's place was a handsome prince with large, beautiful wings.

"Shut your mouth, Katie," said Sam.

"William!" Robert became quite emotional, when he saw that his good friend, Willie the cat, was now a handsome young fairy. William approached his friend.

"You have endured a lot to help me, Robert! I want you to keep the key to Grindle. You may stay as long as you like and when you leave, it is yours to keep for the future."

"We don't have to leave yet, do we?" asked Katie.

Hilga walked up to Grizzard and said, "Okay; the Conjures and I have decided to be easy on you and Gerard. By the way, where is that wimp, Gerard? You can't hide, get out here!"

Gerard, who had finally come into the King's chambers to see what all the fuss was about, stepped out from behind the door.

"I banish you, Grizzard and Gerard, from Grindle!" pronounced Hilga. "But first, I will proclaim myself the Kingdom Wizard. That way I can do everything legally. Anyway, you will spend the rest of your days on a remote island with nothing but palm trees and coconuts. Really not a bad deal, when you think about it, it could be worse, like zapping you to the tundra of some remote part of the world, or . . .”

“Oh, get on with it!” demanded Grizzard.

“HOCUS, POCUS, AWAY FROM ME—TO THE ISLAND OF HA-WAH-HEE!” Hilga waved her arms in the air and stirred up a whirl of wind. Grizzard and Gerard both scrunched their shoulders and squinted as they were picked up into the wind and disappeared. “Poof!”

Brushing off her hands and smoothing her dress, Hilga smiled. “There.”

“Hilga, that island—where is it? I don’t recall any island by that name,” said Sam, the museum expert.

“I had the Conjures search our royal library maps for a far-away place, remote yet comfortable, to send them,” answered Hilga. “I didn’t want them to suffer. Come with me and I will show you.”

They all trekked into the castle, down corridors and around corners to the royal library. It was full of ancient scrolls and maps. On a long table was a map that looked as if it was from the beginning of time. It, too, was on that transparent silver and gold paper. (Or, rather, recycled fairy wings.)

“See, here is that island, along with a bunch of smaller ones.” Hilga pointed to a group of islands west of what looked like, aside from the fact that the map was eons old, what is today called the United States.

“Do you guys see what I’m seeing?” Robert asked, looking at Katie and Sam.

“Ha-Wah-Hee . . . Hawahhee . . . HAWAII!”

Sam threw his hands up in total disbelief, and said, “No, Hilga—I don’t think they will suffer too much.”

Hilga looked at them, bewildered, shrugged and walked to the library terrace and with her black wings outspread, flew out. Robert, Sam and Katie ran to the terrace and looked up. For the first time, Katie noticed Hilga's wings. They were beautiful, with intricate designs. Just above them now sat Hilga, next to Gargoyle. She reached over, patted it affectionately on the head, looked down and said, "Now, William, we will prepare for your crowning ceremony!"

25
The Crown and the Moon

The next week was full of preparation among the fairies for the grand crowning ceremony. While Grindle was buzzing with activity, Robert, Sam and Katie were being shown the ways of the fairy people. William escorted Robert throughout the castle, showing him how up-to-date everything was, while Robert was thinking, compared to what? They visited all the shops in Grindle, the candlestick maker, the baker and the butcher, who, as it turned out, happened to be the man Robert had known as the former Solicitor Redding.

William had some duties to take care of, so he put Robert into the hands of the keeper of the shed fairy wings, who guided him through the recycled wing plant. The keeper fluttering slightly above ground, and Robert, of course, walking.

"You see, when the wings are shed as the fairy grows, they are stored here, until further use, such as paper in books, stationery, medicinal purposes and for replacing window panes in the castle."

Good grief! thought Robert. Then he asked, "Why do fairies shed their wings? And do they grow new ones? I haven't seen anyone here without wings."

"They are shed when the fairy grows," explained the keeper. "They have to have comparable size wings to support them in flight, you know. And, of course, they do grow new ones. It only takes a day or two, otherwise they would have to walk everywhere, and we all know that walking is not good for you."

Robert rolled his eyes. "Oh, I see."

They continued on to the room where the wings were rolled flat for use as pages for books, where the bookbinding process was demonstrated by a "Fairy Bookie."

In the meantime, Katie was taken under "the wings" (so to speak) of the female fairies. They went deep into the forest of giant ferns, orchids, toadstools and vines. They came upon a waterfall and pool beneath, so lovely, that Katie just sighed with wonder. Giant lily pads and flowers floated on top of the pool so clear that pebbles lying on the bottom could be easily seen.

"Come on in, Katie! The water is cool and pleasant."

Katie thought how soft-spoken and peaceful the fairies were. They had dressed her in their flowing garments and pampered her as if she were in an expensive New York spa, one she could never afford, only imagine.

She sat on a large flat rock at the water's edge and lowered her feet into the cool water. Gradually, she immersed her whole body. The rest of the fairies had lifted themselves onto the lily pads to sunbathe. Katie, in turn with awkwardness, tried to lift herself onto a rubbery surface, that kept flipping over, dunking her into the water. She finally made it, with the encouragement and giggles of the other fairies. As she lay on the lily pad, she thought this must be the most wonderful place in the whole world, and yet she couldn't tell anyone back home.

"I could stay here forever," she said aloud as she fell fast asleep.

In the meantime, Sam was nowhere to be seen.

Finally, the time came for Prince William to be crowned King of Grindle. Sam happened to appear for the festive occasion and was dressed accordingly by the royal dresser, as was Robert.

Katie was dressed in flowing robes of iridescent silk, similar to the other female fairies, and her hair was fluffed with a flower garland on her head. She decided she would make an attractive fairy, as she admired herself in the mirror. All she needed were wings.

The square filled with all of Grindle, noisy with chatter and lots of excitement. There were vendors with drinks and fruits, and music was everywhere. Katie, standing with the girls, burst into laughter when she saw Sam and Robert. They were dressed like William, in tunics and tights.

Soon Hilga entered the square, looking quite elegant and proud and quite the Wizard in her newly spun Wizard robe. She carried the famous staff, along with the magic book of the kingdom.

The trumpets blared, announcing the entrance of William's father, who up to now, had been cared for in a special chamber of the castle. He, as some of the three- or four-hundred-year-old fairies did, became somewhat looney. Therefore, a special place was available, with a little padding, for these senior citizens to spend a peaceful and happy time. Hilga motioned for him to stand alongside Robert in the center.

Again, the trumpets blared and William rode in on his beautiful white horse. He dismounted and walked to the center where Hilga was waiting with a silly smile on her face, because this was to be her first performance as Wizard. The trumpets became silent as she motioned for the old king to bring her the crown (which had been yanked off Grizzard's head before he was zapped away), which the king did with the help of his aide.

She touched William gently on his head with her staff and he kneeled before her. She then handed him the Kingdom book and carefully laid the bejeweled crown upon his head. The crowd cheered, along with the blaring of the trumpets. Silver and gold fairy dust and white doves filled the air.

There was dancing and merry-making in the Kingdom. King William was the center of attention, with his new Wizard at his side. Hilga was giddy and cackled a lot.

"Why does she do that? It's like sandpaper up my spine!" Sam scrunched. The Conjures were invited for the festivities and were warmly welcomed by the fairies of Grindle. They were invited to live in the kingdom, instead of the valley, where Grizzard had sent them.

King William approached Robert. "Tonight is the night of the emerging of the new fairies that I told you about before. It only happens once a year. The flower buds at the transport sight in the Fairy Ring are ready to open and it is also a celebration. We will all meet here in the square at midnight, because we have to fly there and since you don't have wings, I've arranged for our giant swans to carry each of you." He then put his hands on Robert's shoulders and said, "Thank you for being here!" He then turned and took flight for his chamber terrace high in the castle top.

"Giant swans?" smirked Sam.

At a half hour before midnight, Robert, Katie and Sam met with William in the square. Around him were three giant swans nestled down to allow for passenger boarding.

"Take a look at those three flying bunches of feathers!" remarked Sam.

"Here, Katie, I'll help you." William took her hand and lifted her onto the first swan.

"Oh! How do I hold on? They're slippery!" she said as she clamped her arms around the swan's neck, making it quack and gag.

"They have feathers on their backs that will wrap around you to hold you on. You won't fall."

Just as he spoke, soft white feathers wrapped around Katie, holding her securely in place. Robert and Sam were also helped onto their transportation and Sam couldn't help but snicker.

"What if they could see us back home!"

King William fluttered his wings and lifted off. The swans stood up and swooped into the air with their passengers. Katie squealed with excitement and all three began to relax and enjoy the flight. As she looked to her side, Sam and Robert's swans caught up to her and they flew in formation, with Katie's swan in the lead. Ahead of her, was William with those great wings gently fluttering and then gliding in the air current. The sky around them was filled with hundreds of flying, fluttering fairies.

The airborne escadrille soon came to a small clearing in the forest. The swans descended to the ground, lowering themselves down with their wings in a slant so their passengers could slide off.

"Follow me," said William. "It's just a little ways now." They came to the clearing of the transport and the huge stones of the Fairy Ring/Stonehenge. They were led into the ring and William motioned them to sit among the flower buds beside him, the Conjures and the other fairies. The large flower buds were a pale yellow with what seemed to be silvery veins through them and were in the shape of a large teardrop, the petals tightly closed.

Hilga stood in the middle of the fairy ring among the

flower buds, and with her staff reached up toward the full moon and slowly moonbeams appeared, along with the sounds of wind chimes. As the moonbeams flooded the flowers with glittering light, fairy dust, from out of nowhere, enveloped each bud in a whirling motion. In minutes, each bud petal began to roll open in a spiral, exposing a small fairy. When all of the petals were opened, the guest observers noticed that the petals were the wings of the fairies. As their wings unfolded, the fairies stood and carefully fluffed each wing until they were fully opened. They then fluttered their exquisite transparent silver and gold wings and flew out of the flower centers. Where up till now was total silence, now there were cheers. The other fairies rose and fluttered up to fly among the new ones.

"Are you crying, Jasper?" frowned Crow.

"No! I just got some fairy dust in my eye!" answered Jasper, who wiped away a tear.

Katie, Sam and Robert stared in disbelief, as they often had done during these past couple of weeks. Suddenly, music came from some of the fairies playing lutes; and other fairies brought, from out of the forest somewhere, platters of food and drink. The food consisted of fruit and berries freshly picked from the forest. The drink was a mixture of honey and milk from the fairy goats.

They feasted and celebrated until dawn. Then as the sun rose, blocking out the moon, the swans swooped down to transport the wingless three back to the castle. Again, they climbed onto the swans' backs and off they soared. The new fairies disappeared into the forest where they were to live until adulthood.

26
Good-bye to Grindle

The next day was the time for Robert, Katie, and Sam to leave Grindle. They had spent some time in paradise and now it was time to return to the real world.

The kingdom fairies, the Conjures, the Royal Wizard, Hilga and His Majesty, King William, gathered once more in the square to bid farewell to their new outside friends and to lead them back to the transport center.

"Robert, with the golden key, you can return to Grindle, because you *will* return someday. In the meantime, it has powers that can be useful to you. Like if you don't like somebody, you can zap them away, just like that. Or if you want to turn someone into a toad, you can . . ."

"No, that's okay, William. I will use it wisely."

Katie bid her new girlfriends good-bye and Sam just stood not saying anything to anyone.

Hilga gave each of them a small bag of fairy dust with her recipes for incantations and what each one would do in case they needed them. She also gave Katie tips on what creatures made the best stew.

"By the way, Hilga," asked Robert, "just what is a warblink?"

"Cackle, cackle . . . there isn't any such thing, but Grizzard didn't know that."

As they approached the Fairy Ring transportation center, Katie looked at some of the trees there. Though she never noticed before, she could swear they had faces.

"Don't take any wooden dracmas!" yelled Conjure Jasper.

"Nickels, you idiot," said Trappy.

Wizard Hilga positioned Robert, Katie, and Sam so they would all be transported at the same time.

"Where would you like to be placed when you return?" she asked.

"Well, I've always hated the long hassles at the airports," said Robert. "Maybe we could bypass all of that, huh?"

"Done," stated Hilga.

"Good-bye for now, my friends," said William, as he hugged each one of them. "You will always be welcome in Grindle." As he stood in all of his majestic grandeur, he motioned for Hilga to begin. She reached her staff to the sky and with a couple of tries, finally brought down one of those lightning bolts. Before she could touch the three of them, Sam stepped aside.

"I'm not going back!"

"What?" Robert and Katie looked at him dumfounded.

"I'm not going back. I'm staying. I have nothing to go back to, just a job in a big city and how could I be content with that when I've found so much here?"

"But, Sam, you can't stay here . . ." Just as Robert spoke, he noticed a beautiful girl fairy step forward and take Sam's hand.

"Oh."

Meantime, the lightning bolt jerked Hilga off of her feet, dragging and whipping her about, as she hung on with both hands. It yanked her up into the sky clear out of sight, then down again, back and forth, in circles, and finally near a tree where she wrapped her legs around the trunk to hang on.

"She has wings, Sam," said Katie.

As Sam looked tenderly at the girl fairy, he said, "I'm going to stay, at least for a year or so, and then when you two come back, I will decide if it will be forever."

"You seem very sure that we will be back."

"Can you think of a better place to spend a vacation?"

"Hey! This lightning bolt is hard to hang onto!" yelled Hilga as she struggled with the whipping bolt.

"Sam is welcome to stay and like he says, we'll see you in a year!" said King William, as he waved good-bye.

The very proud and wizard-like looking Wizard Hilga touched the ground with the bolt and, as Robert and Katie were lifted from the ground, they saw a King, a friend, and a bunch of fairies fade out of sight.

27

To Dream or Not to Dream

Robert awoke from the process of transportation. He looked at Katie, sitting next to him, with her head leaning against the airplane window. It was taking her a little longer to recover. They had been zapped into the last row of the first class section of the jumbo jet en route to New York, thirty-five thousand feet in the air. Robert smiled, thinking that Hilga, in spite of herself, had style.

There were a couple of crew members trying to console a hostess, who was hysterical, saying that when she was serving tea, Robert and Katie appeared out of nowhere right in front of her. A crew member looked at them apologetically and Robert just shrugged his shoulders.

"Robert," Katie sleepily said, as she slowly recovered. "I've had the craziest dream." She looked at the empty seat on the other side of him. "Where's Sam?"

"You weren't dreaming, Katie." Robert reached into his jacket pocket and showed her the "magical golden key."